Barclay V. Head

The Coinage of Lydia and Persia

from the earliest times to the fall of the Dynasty of the Achaemenidae

Barclay V. Head

The Coinage of Lydia and Persia
from the earliest times to the fall of the Dynasty of the Achaemenidae

ISBN/EAN: 9783337287917

Printed in Europe, USA, Canada, Australia, Japan

Cover: Foto ©Andreas Hilbeck / pixelio.de

More available books at **www.hansebooks.com**

THE INTERNATIONAL

NUMISMATA ORIENTALIA.

THE ADVANCED ARTICLES HAVE BEEN UNDERTAKEN BY THE FOLLOWING CONTRIBUTORS:

DR. H. BLOCHMANN.   GENERAL A. CUNNINGHAM.   MR. RHYS DAVIDS.   SIR WALTER ELLIOT.   PROF. JULIUS EUTING.
MR. PERCY GARDNER.   DON PASCUAL DE GAYANGOS.   PROFESSOR GREGORIEF.   MR. F. W. MADDEN.
SIR ARTHUR PHAYRE.   MR. REGINALD S. POOLE.   MR. STANLEY L. POOLE.   MR. E. T. ROGERS.
M. F. DE SAULCY.   M. H. SAUVAIRE.   MR. EDWARD THOMAS.

THE COINAGE OF LYDIA AND PERSIA,

FROM THE EARLIEST TIMES TO THE FALL OF THE DYNASTY OF THE ACHÆMENIDÆ.

BY

BARCLAY V. HEAD,

ASSISTANT-KEEPER OF COINS, BRITISH MUSEUM.

LONDON:

TRÜBNER & CO., 57 AND 59, LUDGATE HILL.

1877.

AUTHOR'S PREFACE.

In a work like the NUMISMATA ORIENTALIA, which is designed to embrace the whole field of Oriental Numismatics, the coinage of the great Persian Empire holds of necessity an avowedly leading position. The famous Persian Darics, "the archers," so frequently alluded to in the history of Greece and of which the influence was often so detrimental to the morality of the Hellenes, form the connecting link between the coinage of the Empire of Croesus on the one hand and that of Alexander the Great on the other. We are thus led to commence with the consideration of the coinage of the kingdom of Lydia, a thorough comprehension of which is primarily desirable for those who would attain to a fuller knowledge of Persian numismatics than is to be gained by a mere contemplation of the types of the coins. The Persian daric is the legitimate successor of the gold stater of Croesus, to whose administrative genius must be ascribed the earliest idea of a double currency based upon the relative values of gold and silver. We are therefore called upon to examine, first of all, the origin of the system of weights in use throughout the East in remote times, and to trace back to their source on the banks of the Euphrates and the Tigris the germs of the weights adopted in Lydia by the ancestors of Croesus, according to which the precious metals were then estimated, and passed from hand to hand as recognised measures of the exchangeable value of all other commodities.

These primitive weight-systems were the basis of the future coinage, not only of Asia, but of European Greece; and Lydia is the border-land, the intermediate territory and link between the East and the West. For this reason I have prefixed to my description of the Lydian coinage an introductory survey of the weight-systems in use throughout the East before the invention of the art of coining. These preliminary remarks are, with some small modifications, extracted from an article which I published in the Numismatic Chronicle (N.S. vol. xv. p. 247 sqq.) "On the ancient electrum coins struck between the Lelantian Wars and the

accession of Darius." The origin and the nomenclature of the Greek systems of
weight is a subject which, until quite lately, has been so much misunderstood both
by metrologists and numismatists, that a recapitulation in the present work of some
of the chief results of the invaluable labours of Mommsen and of Brandis in this
direction will form an appropriate introduction.

But to pass from Metrology to Numismatics. The earliest rude attempts at
coining are undoubtedly the issues of the Sardian mint; but when at a somewhat
later period, probably during the reign of Sadyattes, the artistic influence of the
Greeks of the coast towns began to make itself felt in the Lydian capital, and
when the coins of Lydia are first adorned with the figures of animals, it be-
comes difficult, if not impossible, to draw the line between the coinage of Lydia
and that of the Asiatic Greek cities, and more especially Miletus. In still later
times, during the reign of Croesus, the coinage of Lydia again stands out clearly
marked and easily distinguishable, with its national type, the fore-parts of a Lion
and a Bull face to face. In the intermediate period between Gyges and Croesus,
above alluded to, I have excluded from my Plates all coins not manifestly Lydian
in type, thus giving the preference to the Milesian mint over that of Sardes. In
this attribution to Miletus of many coins sometimes included in the Lydian series,
I am aware that I lay myself open to the charge of having omitted many highly
interesting and important electrum coins; but where a line has to be drawn
between Lydian and Greek, it seems to me to be better to err on the side of
caution, and not to venture upon ascribing positively to Sardes coins which may
just as well have been issued by her great commercial rival Miletus, or by other
wealthy Greek cities of the coast. I have likewise excluded the coins of the
Phocaic standard, struck, with a single exception, by cities in Æolis and the
north-western coast lands, although these were perhaps included in the Lydian
kingdom or tributary to it.

Descending to Persian times, a similar difficulty arises. A strict line of de-
marcation cannot be drawn between Persian and non-Persian. The Persian coinage
proper consists only of the darics and the sigli, and even of these many, if not
the greater number, may have been struck in Asia Minor, rather than in the capital
of the Empire. The darics are, however, inseparable from the double darics, which
latter are probably Asiatic-Greek coins with Persian types. I have consequently
been guided here, as in the case of the Lydian currency, solely by type, accepting

as Persian all coins which bear Persian types, and excluding all such as do not. Of course this is in many cases a purely arbitrary principle of selection, for it cannot be doubted that Persian types were not seldom placed upon some of the coins of Greek cities under the rule more or less direct of Persian satraps; while upon other coins of the same cities this tribute to the supremacy of the Great King was withheld. The former coins are still to all intents and purposes Greek, and not Persian; and in a comprehensive treatise on ancient numismatics they would be inseparable from the series of the coins of the cities to which they respectively belong: but in a work like the present, which deals solely with Oriental numismatics, it is absolutely necessary to bind ourselves down by some such rule as I have here adopted, unless, indeed, we are to restrict ourselves to the royal coinage pure and simple, the darics and the sigli.

The coinage of the Persian satraps has been treated in a similar manner; that is to say, all coins struck by Persian satraps have been excluded, save such, and such only, as bear Persian types; and by Persian types I here mean representations of the Great King.[1]

A treatise on Persian coins in which the money of the satraps is not included may perhaps be likened by some to a nut without the kernel. These coins have, however, been omitted, not from any failure on my part to appreciate at its full value their historical importance, but rather, on the contrary, because I am of opinion that they require a separate monograph.

The history of Lydia and Persia is to so great a degree interwoven with that of Greece, and is, moreover, so generally known, that I have not thought it necessary to give more than the barest outlines requisite for the elucidation of the matter in hand; and in the case of the coins which form the subject of the present article the merest sketch is sufficient, because, owing to the uniformity of type and the lack of inscriptions, it is for the most part impossible to classify them under the several reigns during which they were issued.

I have throughout abstained, as far as possible, from new conjectural attributions, both geographical and chronological, under the conviction that, however plausible such attempts at classifying the coins of the Persian Empire may seem to be, and however intrinsically probable it may be that such and such coins belong to

---

[1] There will be found in the Plates one or two exceptions to this rule, where coins without Persian types form part of a series from which I have not seen my way to exclude them.

such and such reigns or localities, it is better, where there is room for any considerable divergence of opinion among numismatists, to leave the matter undecided. In some cases, however, where the evidence of the coins seemed to be of sufficient weight, I have ventured upon a general opinion as to the locality of certain classes of coins hitherto unattributed.

In conclusion, I have to state my acknowledgments to Mr. Hooft van Iddekinge, of the Hague; Herr Dr. J. Friedlaender, of Berlin; Prof. Dr. H. Brunn, of Munich; and M. Chabouillet, of Paris, for most kindly allowing me to have impressions of coins from the various collections in their charge: also to Mr. J. P. Six, of Amsterdam, not only for impressions of coins from his own cabinet, but for many valuable hints as to the classification of doubtful pieces, as well as for his kindness in bringing to my notice several specimens with which I was previously unacquainted.

BARCLAY V. HEAD.

LONDON, *December*, 1870.

CONTENTS.

THE COINAGE OF LYDIA AND PERSIA.

INTRODUCTION.

SURVEY OF THE WEIGHT-SYSTEMS IN USE FOR GOLD AND SILVER IN THE EARLIEST TIMES.

WHILE the ruder inhabitants of the West were still in search of a method of simplifying their commercial transactions, learning to substitute bronze or iron for the ox and the sheep, *the money* "Pecunia" of primitive times, and the readiest means of barter amid pastoral communities, the precious metals had long since commended themselves to the civilized peoples of the East as being the measure of value least liable to fluctuation, most compact in volume, and most directly convertible.

Untold centuries before the invention of the art of coining, gold and silver were used for the settlement of the transactions of every-day life,[1] either metal having conventionally its crudely defined value in relation to the other. Ingots, or small bars and rings of gold and silver passed from hand to hand estimated by weight, and had to be tested by the scales again and again on every new transfer, being as yet undefined and unsanctioned by any official guarantee of intrinsic value.[2]

[1] For a complete list of all the passages in the Old Testament where uncoined money is mentioned, see Madden in the Num. Chron., 1875, p. 81 sqq.
[2] Smith's Dictionary of Biblical Antiquities, art. 'Money,' by R. S. Poole.

To show how from this rough method of exchange by weight, the precious metals first attained a formal currency, in the true sense of the word, it will be necessary to pass in review the principal weight-systems in use for gold and silver under the great empires of the East, in so far as we are able to follow the authoritative evidence of such Assyrian and Babylonian weights as have been fortuitously preserved to our own times.

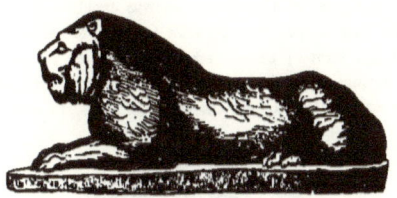

BRONZE LION-WEIGHT FROM NIMRUD.

It is already twenty years since Mr. Norris first published, in the Journal of the Royal Asiatic Society,[1] the Assyrian and Babylonian weights made in the form of Lions and Ducks, the discovery of which, among the ruins of ancient Nineveh, we owe to Mr. Layard. These interesting monuments of remote antiquity, it is almost needless here to repeat, are of the very highest importance to the student of Numismatics, indicating as they do, in the clearest possible manner, the original source of the systems of weight in use throughout Asia Minor and in Greece. The bronze lions and stone ducks are, however, not merely signposts pointing to the banks of the Euphrates and the Tigris; they present us with authentic official documents, inscribed, for the most part, with a double legend, one in Cuneiform characters, the other in Aramaic, generally giving the name of the King of Assyria or of Babylonia in whose reign they were made, together with the number of minæ or of fractions of a mina which each piece originally weighed.

As these weights have lately been all accurately weighed anew, in a balance of precision, I have only to refer the reader to the Ninth Annual Report (1874–5) of the Warden of the Standards, under whose superintendence a complete list of the whole series has been drawn up. It is, therefore, here only necessary to state that the results of this careful reweighing are in the main identical with those arrived at by the late Dr. Brandis, whence it would appear that the mina in use in the ancient Assyrian and Babylonian Empires, during the extended period from B.C. 2000–625, existed in a double form, the heavy mina, falling gradually from a maximum of 1040 grammes [16,068 Eng. grs.] to a minimum of 960

[1] Vol. xvi. p. 215 seq. See also Layard's *Nineveh and Babylon*, p. 601.

[14,832 Eng. grs.], the lighter from about 520 grammes to 460 [8,034—7,107 Eng. grs.]. Dr. Brandis[1] had fixed the weights of those two minæ at 1010 and 505 grammes [15,600 and 7,800 Eng. grs.] respectively, and the evidence of the earliest coins, which must not be neglected in this matter, tends to show that about the time when the Greeks of Asia Minor first became familiar with them, their weights were approximately what Dr. Brandis supposed.

There seem to be but slight grounds, however, in favour of the theory, first broached by Mr. Norris, that the lighter of the two minæ was peculiar to the Babylonian and the heavier to the Assyrian Empire, but it is probable that the use of the heavy mina was more extended than that of the lighter; hence perhaps the addition of an Aramaic inscription on most of the weights belonging to the former, which was probably not only the standard-weight in Assyria, but accepted throughout the whole of Syria, Palestine and Phœnicia.

ASSYRIAN DUCK-WEIGHT (Nimrud).

The lighter mina would nevertheless seem to have been the form more generally adopted in Babylon, although there is nothing to prove that it may not have been also used in Nineveh.

The system according to which the Assyrian and Babylonian talents were subdivided was the sexagesimal, the talent being composed of sixty minæ and the mina of sixty shekels, the shekel being again divided into thirty parts. This sexagesimal system, which pervaded the whole of the Assyrian weights and measures,[2] both of space, of material and of time, in which latter it has maintained itself down to our own age, is for practical employment in weighing and measuring decidedly preferable both to the decimal and the duodecimal, because the number 60 upon which it is founded possesses a far greater power of divisibility than either 10 or 12. The weights of the two talents and their divisions are as follows:—

Heavy Talent	60·600 kilogr.	= 936,000 grs.		
,, Mina	1010	grammes	= 15,600	,,
,, ₆₀ Mina	16·83	,,	= 260	,,
Light Talent	30·300 kilogr.	= 468,000	,,	
,, Mina	505	grammes	= 7,800	,,
,, ₆₀ Mina	8·415	,,	= 130	,,

[1] Brandis, Münz- Mass- und Gewichtswesen in Vorderasien bis auf Alexander den Grossen, p. 45 (Berlin, 1866).
[2] Brandis, p. 7.

Of these two talents the heavy, or so-called Assyrian talent, seems to have passed by land through Mesopotamia and Syria to the Phœnician coast towns and to Palestine, where we find it in use among the Israelites in a somewhat modified form; the Hebrew gold shekel weighing only 253 grs. instead of 260.[1] By the Phœnician traders the heavy talent and its divisions was made known to the Greeks on either side of the Ægean Sea.

The light, or so-called Babylonian talent, on the other hand, found its way from the banks of the Euphrates by land into the kingdom of Lydia, whose capital Sardes was intimately connected on the land side with Babylon, with which it was in constant commercial intercourse.

From these two points, Phœnicia on the one hand and Lydia on the other, the Greeks of Asia Minor received the two units of weight on which the whole fabric of their coinage rests.

How long before the invention of coining these Assyrian and Babylonian weights had found their way westwards, it is impossible to say. It is probable, however, that the Greeks of Asia had long been familiar with them, and that the small ingots of gold and silver, which served the purposes of a currency, were regulated according to the weight of the sixtieth part of the Babylonian mina. It is true that, not bearing the guarantee of the State, it was necessary to put them into the scales and weigh them, like all other materials bought and sold by weight, whenever they passed from the hands of one merchant to those of another; thus although the invention of coining brought with it no essential change in the conditions of commercial intercourse, the precious metals having for ages previously been looked upon as measures of value, it nevertheless very greatly facilitated such intercourse, rendering needless the cumbrous and lengthy process of weighing out the gold or silver to be received in exchange for any given commodity.

In adopting the sixtieth part of the ancient Babylonian mina as their stater or shekel, neither Greeks nor Phœnicians adopted the sexagesimal system in its entirety, but constituted new minæ for themselves, consisting of fifty staters instead of sixty. Thus the Greek stater was identical with the Assyrian and Babylonian sixtieth; but the Greek mina was not identical with the Assyrian mina, since it contained but fifty of these units. On the other hand, the Greek talent contained, like the Assyrian, sixty minæ, though only 3,000 instead of 3,600 staters.

The accepted value of gold as compared with silver was in these times, and for long afterwards, as 13⅓ is to 1;[2] and from this relation of gold to silver the standard by which the latter metal was weighed seems to have been developed in the following manner. The proportion of 13·3 to 1 made it inconvenient to weigh the two metals according to one and

---

[1] Josephus, Arch. xiv. 7, 1, alluding to a weight of gold, says, ἡ δὲ μνᾶ παρ' ἡμῖν ἰσχύει λίτρας δύο καὶ ἥμισυ. The λίτρα here intended is of course the Roman pound = 327·45 gr., therefore 2½ Roman pounds = 818·62 gr.; and as the Hebrew gold shekel was the fiftieth part of the mina, it must have weighed about

16·37 gr., or about 253 English grains.

[2] Herodotus (iii. 89) says 13 to 1, but this is not quite exact, as has been shown by Mommsen, "Note sur le système métrique des Assyriens," which is appended to his Hist. Mon. Rom. ed. Blacas, vol. i. p. 407. See also Brandis, p. 62 seq.

the same standard, as in that case a given weight in gold would not have been exchangeable for a round number of bars of silver, but for thirteen and one third of such bars; hence, in order to facilitate the exchange of the two metals, the weight of the silver stater was raised above or lowered beneath that of the gold stater, in order that the gold sixtieth might be easily convertible into a round number of silver staters.

Now the sixtieth part of the heavy gold Assyrian mina was a piece weighing about 260 grs. Dividing this piece again by sixty, we obtain a minute gold piece weighing only 4·3 grs.; if we multiply this by 13·3, the proportionate value of silver to gold, we arrive at a unit in silver of about 57 grains. Thus arose the silver drachm introduced by the Phœnicians into Greece, upon which the so-called Græco-Asiatic or Phœnician silver-standard is based. According to the sexagesimal system, its value was that of the sixtieth part of the sixtieth of the gold mina. Four of these silver sixtioths formed a piece of metal weighing about 230 grs. (maximum). This became the stater of the Phœnician silver-standard, and as fifteen of these silver staters go to form one gold sixtieth, this standard has been designated by Brandis as the Fifteen-stater standard.

The people of Lydia, adopting a different method, arrived at a silver stater of a different weight. We have seen that at Sardes the light or Babylonian gold mina, travelling by land, had become domesticated. The sixtieth of this mina, weighing 130 grs., multiplied by 13·3, yields about 1729 grs. of silver. Applying to this silver-weight a decimal division, they arrived at a convenient silver stater of about 170 grs., and as ten of these pieces are equivalent to one gold sixtieth, this standard has been called by Brandis the Ten-stater standard.

Both the Fifteen- and the Ten-stater standards are thus in reality based upon one and the same unit, viz. a piece of about 57 grs. This is the third part of the stater of 170 grains, and the fourth part of the stater of 230 grs. We therefore see why the former of these staters is regularly divided into three, and the latter into two and four parts.[1]

As the Phœnicians had penetrated everywhere, establishing, with their accustomed enterprise, their factories on almost every coast, they soon discovered the metallic wealth of the land, and began to work for the first time the veins of silver which had lain for ages unsuspected in the mountains. Hence, little by little, the Phœnician silver weight became widely known throughout the Greek world. The Babylonic silver standard, on the other hand, outside the kingdom of Lydia, was hardly known at all until after the Persian conquest, when it was adopted for the silver currency of the Empire and its dependent satraps.

The Greeks, however, when they first struck coins of silver, did not everywhere adopt the prevalent Phœnician standard. Chalcis and Eretria, perhaps the most important commercial cities of European Greece, had established, as early as the eighth century B.C., an active maritime trade with the opposite coasts of Asia Minor, and from these coasts they received the Babylonian gold mina with its sixtieth, viz. 130 grains. As there was little or no gold

[1] Brandis, p. 58.

on their own side of the sea, while silver, on the other hand, flowed into Euboea from her colonies in the mining districts of Macedon and Thrace, the cities of that island transferred to silver the standard with which they had become familiar in their commerce with the Ionian towns, and on this Babylonic gold standard they struck their earliest silver staters, weighing 130 grains. Their example was soon followed by Corinth and Athens, and the Babylonian origin of this weight was lost sight of by the Greeks, and the name of the Euboic talent was applied by them to the old Babylonian gold weight; all coins, whether gold or silver, struck not only in Greece, but in the East, on this weight, being said to follow the Euboic standard. The name of the Babylonic standard, nevertheless, remained in use for the Lydian and Persian silver weight,[1] which had been developed by the Lydians out of the light gold mina. By the Babylonic talent the Greeks therefore understood a silver standard, the stater of which weighed 170 grs.; while by the Euboic talent they understood a standard used either for silver or gold, the stater of which weighed 130 grains.

About the end of the eighth century B.C., or in other words about the time when the Greeks of Asia Minor or the Lydians first hit upon the idea of stamping the bars of metal with official marks as guarantees of their weight and value, the following were therefore the weights generally current in commercial intercourse:—

(a.)

(i.) The 60th of the heavy Assyrian mina in gold, weighing 260 grains.

This weight had found its way through Syria and Phœnicia to the coasts of Asia Minor. The earliest coins of this class are said to have been issued at Phocæa. Hence the earliest gold staters of 256 grains (maximum), with their subdivisions, have been designated as of the Phocaic standard.

(ii.) The corresponding silver piece of 230 grains, fifteen of which were equal in value to one Phocaic gold stater.

This weight, which was also of Phœnician transmission, was adopted by many of the coast towns of Asia Minor for their silver currency. The actual weight of the coins of this standard seldom came up to the normal weight of 230 grains, 220 grains being about the average. As the earliest coins of this weight were issued by Greek cities of Asia Minor, it has obtained the name of the Græco-Asiatic standard. Brandis calls it the Fifteen-stater standard.

---

[1] This is clear from the statement of Herodotus (iii. 89) concerning the revenues of the Great King, where he gives the sums paid in silver by the nineteen satrapies in Babylonian talents, while the twentieth (the Indian), he says, paid in Euboic talents of gold. Concerning this whole passage, vide Mommsen, Hist. Mon. Rom. ed. Blacas, vol. i. p. 27 sq.; Brandis, p. 63; Hultsch, p. 276.

(iii.) The weight adopted by Pheidon, when, some time before the middle of the seventh century, he first instituted a mint in the island of Ægina.

> This appears to be only a degradation of the Phœnician silver standard,[1] the maximum weight of the earliest Æginetic staters being as high as 212 grs., though the average weight is not more than 190 grs. The Æginetic standard in the earliest times was prevalent throughout the Peloponnesus, in the Chalcidian colonies in Italy and Sicily, in Crete, on the Cyclades, especially Coos, Naxos, and Siphnos, and even in certain towns in Asia Minor, among which Teos and perhaps Cyme may be mentioned, as well as in many other localities which need not here be particularized.

(β.)

(iv.) The 60th of the light Babylonian gold mina, weighing 130 grains.

> This weight found its way by land from the banks of the Euphrates to Sardes, and from Sardes probably through Samos to the important commercial cities of Euboea, Chalcis and Eretria, where silver coins of 130 grs. were first issued. Whether used for silver as in Greece, or for gold as in the East, this weight went by the name of the Euboic standard.

(v.) The corresponding silver piece of 170 grains, ten of which were equal in value to one Euboic gold stater of 130 grains.

> This weight, being first met with in the silver coinage of the Lydians, who had doubtless derived it from Babylon, retained its original name, and was known as the Babylonic silver standard. It has been designated by Brandis as the Ten-stater standard.

---

[1] Brandis ingeniously develops the Æginetic silver standard out of the electrum stater of 220 grs. in the following manner. In the first place he supposes the electrum stater to contain about one-third of silver; he then takes what remains of pure gold, viz. about 146 grs., the silver equivalent of which, according to the recognized proportionate value of the two metals, is 1941 grains of silver or just 10 Æginetic silver staters of 194 grs.

ELECTRUM.

Besides gold and silver, a third precious metal was recognized by the ancients, which as early as the time of Sophocles was known by the name of electrum. It was also called white gold, and appears to have been always looked upon as a distinct metal.[1]

Electrum was obtained in large quantities from the washings of the Pactolus, and from the mines on Tmolus and Sipylus. It was composed of about three parts of gold and one part of silver. It therefore stood in an entirely different relation to silver from that of pure gold, the latter being to silver as 13·3 is to 1, while electrum was about 10 to 1.[2]

This natural compound of gold and silver possessed several advantages for purposes of coining over gold, which, as might have been expected, were not overlooked by a people endowed in so high a degree with commercial instincts as were the inhabitants of the coast towns of Asia Minor. In the first place, it was more durable, being harder and less subject to wear; secondly, it was more easily obtainable, being found in large quantities in the immediate neighbourhood; and, lastly, standing as it did in the simple relation of 10 to 1 as regards silver, it rendered needless the use of a different standard of weight for the two metals, enabling the authorities of the mints to make use of one set of weights and a decimal system easy of comprehension and simple in practice.

On this account electrum was weighed according to the silver standard, and the talent, the mina, and the stater of electrum were consequently equivalent to ten talents, ten minæ, or ten staters of silver of the same weight.

The weight of the electrum stater in each town or district thus depended upon the standard which happened to be in use there for silver bullion or silver bar-money, the practice of the new invention of stamping metal for circulation being in the first instance only applied to the more precious of the two metals, the electrum stater representing, in a conveniently small compass, a weight of uncoined silver, or silver in the shape of bars or ingots, ten times as bulky and ten times as difficult of transport. Once, however, in general use, the extension to silver and to gold of the new invention of coining could not be long delayed.

As the standards according to which bullion silver was weighed were various in various localities, having been developed, as we have seen above, by different methods out of the sixtieth

[1] It does not appear, however, that money coined in this metal was called by a different name from that used to designate pure gold. Thus in the Attic inscriptions (Corp. Inscr. Att. ed. Kirchhoff, vol. I. no. 301) we find χρυσοῦ στατῆρες Κυζικηνοί or χρυσίου Κυζικηνοῦ στατῆρες, in these cases electrum, and Δαρεικοῦ χρυσίου στατῆρες, in this case gold. The real distinction lay, not in the name of the metal, but in the specifications Κυζικηνός or Δαρεικός, just as in English we speak of German silver.

[2] This applies only to the period when gold was as 13·3 is to 1. In later times, when gold had fallen to 10 : 1, electrum would only be about 7½ : 1, as is evident from Demosthenes's valuation of the Cyzicene stater at 28 Attic drachms.

parts of the heavy and light Babylonian gold minæ, so also were the earliest electrum staters of different weights, depending everywhere upon silver, and not upon gold. Consequently, as might have been expected, we meet with electrum coins of the Phœnician, the Æginetic, the Babylonic and the Euboic systems.[1] The coins of the so-called Phocaic system stand on a somewhat different footing. This standard, as we have seen above, was not a silver standard, but a gold one, based upon the 60th of the heavy Babylonian gold mina weighing about 260 grains; hence the electrum coins which follow this standard are clearly distinguishable, not only by their weight, but by their colour, from the electrum of the four silver standards. Whether they ought to be included under the heading of Electrum is almost a question; for the majority of these coins approach more nearly to gold in colour, and they were probably intended to circulate as gold,—the metal of which they are composed not being the natural electrum, as found in Lydia, but an artificial compound, the use of which, as representing gold, may have been a source of some profit to the State.

[1] Num. Chron. 1875, pp. 254 sqq.

PART I.

LYDIA.

The preceding review of the principal systems of weight used in the East and in Asia Minor for the precious metals, circulating simply as such and not as coins, leads us to the more immediate subject of this article, the COINAGE OF LYDIA AND PERSIA.

Lydia, as Prof. E. Curtius remarks in his History of Greece, was in ancient times "the western outpost of the Assyrian World-empire"; and when this empire fell into decay, Lydia, following the example of Media and Babylonia, threw off the yoke she had worn for five centuries, and under a new dynasty, the Mermnadæ, entered upon a new and independent course of national life. The policy of the new rulers of the country, who were originally Carian mercenaries, was to extend the power of Lydia towards the West, to obtain possession of towns on the coast, and thus to found a naval power, in which the boldness and enterprise of the Greek might be, as it were, engrafted upon the spirit of commercial activity which the natives of Lydia possessed in common with all people of Semitic race.

PERIOD I. REIGNS OF GYGES AND ARDYS.

With this object, Gyges, the Founder of the dynasty of the Mermnadæ, who ascended the throne shortly before B.C. 700, established a firm footing on the Hellespont, where, under his auspices, the city of Abydos was founded.[1] His next step was to secure, if possible, the dominion of the entire Ionian coast. In this project he met with considerable success, but did not live to see the realization of his dreams.

His successor Ardys, B.C. 660–637,[2] prosecuted the war with the Ionians with uninterrupted ardour, and would doubtless have succeeded in uniting the whole coast-line under the dominion of Sardes, had not the invasion of the Cimmerian hordes called off his forces to protect his own dominions from the incursions of the Barbarians.

---

[1] Strabo, xiii. p. 590: "Ἄβυδος δὲ Μιλησίων ἐστὶ κτίσμα, ἐπιτρέψαντος Γύγου τοῦ Λυδῶν βασιλέως· ἦν γὰρ ὑπ᾽ ἐκείνῳ τὰ χωρία καὶ ἡ Τρωὰς ἅπασα.

[2] Maspero. Hist. anc. des peuples de l'orient, Paris, 1875, p. 483.

To the reign of Gyges, the Founder of the new Lydian Empire, as distinguished from the Lydia of more remote antiquity, which, as we have soon above, was closely united with the Empire of Assyria, must be ascribed the earliest essays of the art of coining. The wealth of Gyges in the precious metals may be inferred from the munificence of his gifts to the Delphic shrine, consisting of golden mixing cups and silver vessels, and amounting to a mass of gold and silver such as the Greeks had never before seen collected together.[1] It is in conformity with the whole spirit of a monarch such as Gyges, whose life's work it was to extend his empire towards the West, and at the same time to keep in his hands the lines of communication with the East, that from his capital Sardes, situate on the slopes of Tmolus and on the banks of the Pactolus, both rich in gold, he should send forth along the caravan routes of the East, into the heart of Mesopotamia, and along the river-valleys of the West down to the sea, his native Lydian ore gathered from the washings of the Pactolus and from the diggings on the hill-sides. This precious metal he issued in the form of ingots stamped with a mark to guarantee their weight and value. For his commerce with Babylon by land a crude lump of electrum was issued weighing 168·4 grains and consequently worth, at the proportion of 10:1 to silver, exactly one-fifth of the Babylonian silver mina of 8420 grains.[2] On the other hand, for dealings with the Ionian coast towns, where the Babylonian silver mina was unknown, it was necessary to put into circulation an electrum stater of the weight of 224 grains, five of which would exchange for one Græco-Asiatic silver mina of 11200 grains.[3] Thus then the first issues of the Sardian mint went forth in two opposite directions, embracing both East and West in the circle of their far-reaching currency. The commercial instincts of the Lydians guiding the policy of the State even in times of war, for the border-feuds with the Ionian territory by no means interfered with the intercourse between Greeks and Lydians, as is evident from the care taken by the Lydian kings to conduct the war with extreme moderation, all Temples of the gods and even human habitations being spared in the struggle for hegemony between Lydia and Ionia.

To the reigns of Gyges and Ardys, B.C. 700–637, may probably be attributed all such staters of electrum as bear no type,—the obverse being plain and the reverse marked with three deep incuse depressions, the one in the centre oblong, and the others square,—together with certain similar smaller coins which appear to represent the $\frac{1}{3}$, the $\frac{1}{6}$, the $\frac{1}{12}$ and the $\frac{1}{24}$ parts of the larger of the two staters.

The following is a description of the earliest issues of the Sardian mint, none of which would appear to be later than the reign of Ardys.

---

[1] Curtius, Gr. Gesch. Bd. i. p. 466, Berlin, 1857. Herod. i. 14: ὁ δὲ χρυσὸς οὗτος καὶ ὁ ἄργυρος, τὸν ὁ Γύγης ἀνέθηκε, ὑπὸ Δελφῶν καλένται Γυγάδας ἐπὶ τοῦ ἀναθέντος ἐπωνυμίην.

[2] There was another form of the Babylonian silver mina, weighing 8645 grs., but this does not appear to have come into use until Persian times, the Persian siglos weighing 86·45 grs. and the stater 172·9. It is therefore convenient to distinguish this heavier form by the name of the Perso-Babylonic silver mina.

[3] The full weight of the stater and mina of this standard were 230 and 11500 grs.

ELECTRUM.

(i) BABYLONIC STANDARD.

Stater.

WEIGHT.	OBVERSE.	REVERSE.
166·8	Plain (*Typus fasciatus*).	Three incuse depressions, that in the centre oblong, the others square, within the central oblong a Fox ?? running left.
		[Brit. Mus. Plate I. 1.]

(ii) GRÆCO-ASIATIC STANDARD.

Stater.

219	Plain (*Typus fasciatus*).	Similar: the devices contained in all three incuses visible: in the centre a Fox, in the upper square an animal's head (? Stag's), in the lower an ornament **✕**.
		[Lenormant, Monnaies Royales de la Lydie, p. 1.]

Half-Stater.

105·8	Plain (*Typus fasciatus*).	Three incuse depressions: that in the centre oblong, the others square. Double struck.
		[Brit. Mus Plate I. 2.]

Sixth.

37	Plain (*Typus fasciatus*).	Two incuse squares of different sizes.
		[Brit. Mus. Plate I. 3.]

Twelfth.

18	Plain (*Typus fasciatus*).	Incuse square.
		[Mus. Luynes. Plate I. 4.]

Twenty-Fourth.

9	Plain (*Typus fasciatus*).	Incuse square.
		[Brit. Mus. Plate I. 5.]

In the Fox, which is more or less visible in the central incuse on the staters both of the Babylonic and Græco-Asiatic standards, M. F. Lenormant recognizes a symbol of the Lydian Dionysus, whose name Bassareus may be connected with the word Bassara or Bassaris, a Fox.[1] From the Temple treasury of this god the earliest coins of Sardes may therefore have been issued.

The example, having been once set by Sardes, of stamping pieces of electrum with punchmarks containing small devices as a guarantee of their weight, was soon followed by her haughty rival. Miletus, the wealthiest commercial city on the whole Asiatic coast, and the artistic Greek

---

[1] Stephanus, Thesaurus, s.v.

was quick to adopt and to beautify the Lydian invention. The first issues of the Milesian Mint, while retaining the form of incuse peculiar to the Lydian money, bore upon the obverse the figure of a Lion generally in a recumbent attitude with head turned back. Ephesus, Cyme, and another city which has not been identified with certainty, soon followed suit, striking electrum staters with their respective types, the stag, the fore-part of a horse, and a bull; the Ephesian stater bearing in addition to its type an inscription in archaic characters which has been read by Mr. Newton (Num. Chron. N.S. vol. x. p. 237), ΑΜΒΖΙΜΞΗΟΝΞΑΦ, "I am the token or coin of the Bright One" (*i.e.* Artemis). This stater, now in the collection of the Bank of England, is the earliest inscribed coin known.

All these cities, in applying the Lydian invention, restricted their first issues to electrum, which they coined according to the Graeco-Asiatic or Phoenician silver standard, the average weight of the stater of which is about 220 grains.

Samos alone adopted a different standard,[1] and struck her electrum coins according to the light Babylonian gold mina, the stater of which weighed about 130 grains; and as we know that this standard was in use for silver in the island of Euboea, there is every reason to suppose that we possess in this circumstance the key to the otherwise anomalous fact of electrum and gold being weighed according to one and the same standard. To account therefore for the weight of the Samian electrum stater, we must suppose that the Euboic silver mina was in use in that island as well as in Euboea; but whether Chalcis originally derived it from Samos, or Samos from Chalcis, it is impossible to say with certainty.

PERIOD II. REIGNS OF SADYATTES AND ALYATTES.

The second period of the coinage of Lydia extends from the accession of Sadyattes in B.C. 637, to that of Croesus in 568.[2] Sadyattes, the son of Ardys, after the Cimmerian hordes had been at length finally expelled from Asia Minor, found himself at liberty again to turn his attention to the West. He laid siege to Miletus, and year after year wasted her fertile lands; but, owing to the obstinate resistance of the citizens, was never permitted to enter their walls as a conqueror. He was succeeded by his son Alyattes, who continued for some years longer the blockade of the great Ionian city, but with no more fortunate result. Under their Tyrant Thrasybulus, the Milesians, though indeed hard pressed for food, contrived to deceive the Lydian monarch as to the extent of their remaining resources, and finally he was induced to abandon all hopes of subduing them by force of arms, and to conclude with them a treaty of alliance after a war which had lasted for the space of eleven years.

During this time of hardship and impoverishment it is probable that Miletus ceased to issue

---

[1] Metrol. Not. on Anc. El. pp. 26-27; Num. Chron. 1875, p. 270 sq.

[2] The dates here assigned to the Lydian kings can only be looked upon as approximate. Chronologists are still at variance respecting them.

staters, and that her coinage was restricted to the smaller denominations such as Thirds and Sixths, which would suffice for her domestic necessities; the mintage of the Græco-Asiatic stater being transferred to her ally Chios and to other coast towns. Among these electrum staters of the second period, which are all probably subsequent to the siege of Miletus, specimens have come down to us of Chios, Clazomenæ and Chalcis in Ionia, and of Lampsacus and Abydos in the North. The reverses of these staters are no longer of the primitive Lydian type, but exhibit the ordinary incuse square sometimes divided into four quarters. The character of the work upon the obverses of these later coins is also more advanced than that of the extremely archaic staters of Miletus, Ephesus and Cyme mentioned above (p. 13).

In the mean time the coinage of the Lydian Empire itself seems to have undergone some modification. The influence of the arts of Ionia began to be felt in Sardes, and instead of the uniform plain surface of metal, relieved only by irregular streaks, which characterizes the coins of the reigns of Gyges and Ardys, those of a somewhat later period, which I would give conjecturally to the time of Sadyattes and Alyattes, are adorned with types after the Greek fashion, and, if we may judge by their style, are the works of Greek engravers in the employment of the Lydian monarch. It is indeed impossible to distinguish them with absolute certainty from the coins of the Greek coast towns, and there will always be some difference of opinion among Numismatists as to which are Greek and which are Lydian. It is only by comparing them with the coinage of Crœsus, which as I shall show later on is well defined and uniform in type, that we are able to set aside from the numerous types of the Græco-Asiatic electrum stater of this period one or two specimens as Lydian. The money of Crœsus, both of gold and silver, is distinguished by one invariable device, which is the same on all the denominations, from the gold stater to the smallest silver coin—the fore-parts of a Lion and Bull; and this same device, or at any rate something of a similar nature, would seem to have been the special mark of the Lydian currency from the time of Sadyattes or thereabouts. This imperial device—the Arms, so to speak, of the city of Sardes—was doubtless, like the types of all the earliest coins of Greek cities, of religious origin, and is therefore to be distinguished from that of the Royal Persian money of Darius and his successors, which was adorned with the effigy of the Great King himself.

The only stater of the Græco-Asiatic standard which in my judgment is undoubtedly Lydian, and of the time of Sadyattes or Alyattes, is one which may be thus described.

ELECTRUM.

GRÆCO-ASIATIC STANDARD.

Stater.

WEIGHT.	OBVERSE.	REVERSE.
215·4	Fore-parts of Lion and Bull turned away from each other and joined by their necks.	Three incuse depressions, that in the centre oblong, the others square.

[Munich. Plate I. 6.]

The following I should prefer to attribute to Miletus during the time of her prosperity before the wars with Lydia, rather than to Sardes, notwithstanding the occurrence of the Fox upon the reverse of the Half-stater. The Lion on the obverse is the principal type, and by this we must be guided in our attribution. The Stag's head and the Fox on the reverse of the Half-stater may simply indicate that the coin, although issued from the Milesian Mint, was current both in Ephesus and Sardes.

ELECTRUM.

GRÆCO-ASIATIC STANDARD.

Staters.

WEIGHT.	OBVERSE.	REVERSE.
215·3	Fore-part of Lion, right, star above forehead.	Three incuse depressions, that in the centre oblong, the others square.
	[Brit. Mus. Num. Chron. N.S. vol. xv. pl. vii. 3.]	
217·8	Lion recumbent right, looking left.	Similar, but incuses containing ornaments.
	[Brit. Mus. Brandis, p. 402, incorrectly described as a Chimæra.]	
218	Lion recumbent left, looking right, within an oblong frame.	Three incuse depressions, that in the centre oblong, the others square but irregularly formed.
	[Cabinet de France, Brandis, p. 394.]	

Half-stater.

107	Lion recumbent right, looking left, within an oblong frame.	Similar, but each sinking containing a type; the upper square a Stag's head, the central oblong a Fox walking l., the lower square an ornament ✕.
	[Brit. Mus. Num. Chron. N.S. vol. xv. pl. viii. 4.]	

Third.

72	Lion recumbent left, looking right.	Two incuse squares, containing respectively ✕ and N.
	[Cabinet de France, Brandis, p. 394.]	

The Thirds, Sixths, etc., having on the obverse the head of a Lion surmounted by a star, are undoubtedly Milesian, and represent, in my opinion, the later period of the activity of the Milesian Mint; for the Milesian electrum would seem to have undergone some alteration in its value, if, as is generally the case, the numerous countermarks which occur on nearly all the coins to which I am now alluding are any indication of a reissue. This alteration in the value of the Milesian electrum, and if of the Milesian probably also of the Lydian electrum, may be in part the effect of the rise in importance of Phocæa, and of the first issue of a comparatively pure gold coinage on the so-called Phocaic standard, a coinage which would naturally serve still further to depreciate the value of the less-pure Lydian metal, already perhaps circulating somewhat above its intrinsic value. It is not, therefore, surprising if we notice about this time (circ. B.C. 600) a general cessation of the pale electrum coinage of Lydia and the Greek coast towns, and on the other hand a corresponding extension of the coinage of dark-coloured electrum, probably circulating as gold, according to the Phocaic system.

Now between the cessation of the pale electrum coinage shortly after the Milesian war and the accession of Crœsus in B.C. 568, there is a period of about half a century during which the city of Phocæa seems to have obtained a considerable increase of power and influence, more especially upon the sea. It may therefore be considered as certain that the rise and extension of the Phocaic standard coincides with this period, during which the Phocæans, owing in part perhaps to the troubles of Miletus, are said to have been supreme upon the sea (θαλαττοκρατεῖν). This period, according to Eusebius (Chron. ii. ed. Mai, p. 331), lasted forty-four years, commencing from B.C. 575. It has, however, been proved that this date is erroneous, and that the commencement of the Phocæan Thalassocracy should be placed in the year B.C. 602.[1] From this time until that of Crœsus, the influence of Phocæa, both by sea and land, appears to have been sufficiently strong to carry through a reform in the gold currency of the greater part of the Asiatic coast lands; and it is therefore worthy of remark that the staters of the Phocaic standard, as originally issued by the cities of Phocæa, Teos, Cyzicus, and others, are not of the pale-coloured electrum of the old Milesian and Lydian standard, but are of comparatively pure gold, and that they follow the standard afterwards adopted by Crœsus for his royal gold coinage, the Phocaic stater weighing 256 grains, which is, allowing for a slight per-centage of alloy, just double the value of the staters of Crœsus. This is a coincidence which leads me to infer that the cities which took part with Phocæa in the issue of this new coinage intended their money to circulate as gold, and not as electrum, and that, therefore, although they retained the globular form of coin with which the Asiatic Greeks had been long familiar, they at the same time selected the old Babylonic gold standard with its sixtieth of 260 grains for their new gold stater.

It has been generally supposed that the Phocaic coinage was contemporary with the Milesian, and that Miletus, contemporaneously with her electrum of 220 grains, struck gold on the Phocaic standard of 250 grains (Brandis, p. 395); and the stater attributed to that city, with the type of the Lion's head described below, has even been considered by Burgon to be the oldest of all Greek coins. In my judgment both the Milesian origin and the supposed high antiquity of this piece are exceedingly doubtful. The style in which the Lion's head is executed differs essentially from that of the early coins of Miletus, and may be called barbaric rather than archaic. It bears a much closer resemblance, on the other hand, to the Lions' heads upon the staters of Crœsus, but is even more roughly executed. Now, as I have shown above, it was from the first the policy of the Mermnadæ in Lydia to render the coinage of Sardes conformable, on the one hand, to that of the wealthiest and most important of the Greek coast towns with which Sardes carried on an active

[1] Goodwin, " De potentiæ veterum gentium maritimæ epochis apud Eusebium," Göttingen, 1855.

commercial intercourse, and, on the other, with the vast empires of the interior. I would therefore
suggest that the gold stater with the Lion's head may be also Lydian, and that it may represent
an endeavour on the part of Alyattes to assimilate his currency, not only in value, but also in
fabric, to that of the Ionic coast towns ; and as during the latter part of his reign the influence of
Phocæa seems to have been predominant, and the Phocaic gold stater to have been little by little
ousting the pale electrum, so Alyattes, in order to facilitate intercourse with the Greek cities
which had adopted this standard, may have struck the gold staters, which may be thus described, of the fabric and weight of those of Phocæa.

GOLD.

Phocaic Standard.

Stater.

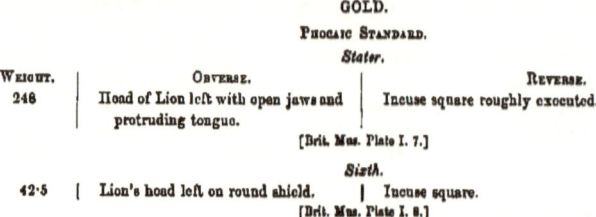

Weight.	Obverse.	Reverse.
246	Head of Lion left with open jaws and protruding tongue.	Incuse square roughly executed.

[Brit. Mus. Plate I. 7.]

Sixth.

42·5	Lion's head left on round shield.	Incuse square.

[Brit. Mus. Plate I. 8.]

The attribution of these coins to Sardes rather than Miletus is of more importance than
might be at first imagined, since it enables us to define within more reasonable limits the
territory over which the influence of Phocæa extended, while at the same time we are no
longer compelled to suppose that Miletus suddenly changed the standard of her coinage or
issued contemporaneously coins of two different systems; for it is probable that during the
period to which I propose to attribute the issue of Phocaic gold, viz. about B.C. 600–560,
Miletus was still striking Thirds and Sixths on the Asiatic standard, although doubtless the
activity of her mint had been much affected by her wars with Lydia.

The territory over which the influence of the Phocaic gold coinage extended would seem
therefore, judging from the coins which have come down to us, to have included the district
from Teos northwards to the shores of the Propontis, together with, in all probability, the islands
of Lesbos and Thasos on the opposite coast of Thrace.

The following is a list of the Phocaic gold staters which are to be found in various collections. Among them is the stater with the Lion's head, described more fully above.[1]

GOLD.

Phocaic Standard.

Staters.

Weight.	City.	Obverse.	Reverse.
254	Phocæa.	Seal right, beneath ☉.	Two incuse squares of different sizes.

[Munich. Num. Chron. N.s. vol. xv. pl. x. 6.]

[1] It is unnecessary here to enumerate the smaller coins of the same system, of which a complete list will be found in my paper in
the Numismatic Chronicle, N.s. vol. xv. p. 292.

WEIGHT.	CITY.	OBVERSE.	REVERSE.
256	Teos.	TƧOM Griffin's head.	Small incuse square.
		[Munich. Brandis, p. 397.]	
248	Sardes.	Head of Lion l. with open jaws and protruding tongue.	Incuse square roughly executed.
		[Brit. Mus. Plate I. 7.]	
252	Cyzicus.	Tunny fish between two fillets.	Two incuse squares, the larger one containing zigzag ornaments, the smaller a Scorpion or Cray-fish (ἀστακός ?).
		[Brit. Mus. Num. Chron. N.S. vol. xv. pl. x. 7.]	
252·7	Zeleia.	Chimæra walking left.	Two incuse squares of different sizes.
		[Brit. Mus. Num. Chron. N.S. vol. xv. pl. x. 9.]	
252	Thrace or Thasos.	Centaur carrying off a nymph.	Deep incuse square quartered.
		[Bank of England. Num. Chron. N.S. vol. xv. pl. x. 11.]	

That Alyattes should have added to the Lydian electrum coinage a gold piece of the Phocaic standard, in order to bring his currency into harmony with that of the north-western coast district, is just what might have been expected of a prince whose ability and good fortune were such that, after proving himself able to maintain intact the eastern boundary of his kingdom, the river Halys, in the face of an invasion led by the allied kings of Media and Babylonia, he again turned his attention with renewed vigour to the sea-coast, where he endeavoured by force of arms, as well as by peaceful means, to strengthen the Lydian power.

His two sons Crœsus and Adramytes were sent to uphold their father's authority in Mysia, where, at the head of the great gulf which bore its name, opposite the island of Lesbos, the city of Adramytteum was founded, as a Lydian commercial settlement, in the heart of the district over which the Phocaic gold coinage prevailed. For the space of nearly a quarter of a century, Crœsus, as his father's viceroy, ruled over the north-western portion of Asia Minor, during which period of uninterrupted prosperity the commercial intercourse between Sardes and the sea was, in this direction, brought to its fullest development.

That the gold coinage of Phocœa and the north-western portion of Asia Minor possessed advantages over the pale electrum of Sardes, as being more widely acceptable in foreign commerce, must have soon become apparent to a man possessed of the insight and sagacity of Crœsus, to whose influence it is doubtless owing that the Phocaic gold stater was engrafted upon the ancient electrum currency of his father's dominions. When therefore, in B.C. 568, he succeeded to the throne of Sardes, one of his first objects was to carry through and develope the monetary reform which had already been commenced by the introduction, during the reign of Alyattes, of the Phocaic stater. No man of his time knew the mission of gold as Crœsus did, and to substitute an imperial currency of pure gold which might be universally accepted both in Greece and in

Asia, instead of the electrum money of ancient times, was a stroke of policy calculated in the highest degree to raise the prestige of the Lydian power in a commercial point of view over that of any other state.

PERIOD III. REIGN OF CRŒSUS; HIS MONETARY REFORMS.

When Crœsus ascended the throne of the Mermnadæ, one of his first acts was to propitiate the Hellenes on either side of the sea by magnificent offerings of equal value to the great sanctuaries of Apollo both at Delphi and at Branchidæ.[1] He next proceeded to obtain a recognition of his sovereignty from all the Greek cities of Ionia, of Æolis, and of Mysia, which one after another fell into his hands, and were for the most part peaceably incorporated into the Lydian Empire, to which they were in future to pay tribute, retaining at the same time their full autonomy. Henceforth, as Prof. Curtius remarks,[2] "the burdensome stoppages between the coast and the interior were removed, and a free interchange took place of the treasures of the East and West. All the ports were open to Crœsus, and all the maritime population at his disposal; all the industry and sagacity, all the art and science, which had been developed on this coast, were ready to serve him in return for his money. . . . . By his resolution and sagacity he had realized the objects of the policy of the Mermnadæ, which had been pursued with rare consistency through five generations of their house. His empire, acknowledged as one of the great powers of Asia, had been the first among the latter to obtain possession of the sea-coast, and to overcome the opposition between the Hellenes and the Barbarians. Beside being a land power of the interior, feared in all Asia, and based on a well-defined and richly endowed system of landed property, on sturdy popular forces and an efficient army, it included the splendid succession of flourishing sea-ports; and the Pactolus unceasingly rolled his golden sands before the portals of the royal citadel of Sardes."

Crœsus, as we have seen, on his accession found two electrum staters current in his kingdom in addition to the Phocaic gold stater, which he had himself lately introduced; one weighing 220 grains for commerce with Miletus and the Greek cities which had adopted the Milesian standard, and another weighing 168 grains for the purposes of the trade by land with the interior and with Babylon.

Both these electrum staters he abolished at a single stroke, and in their place a double currency consisting of pure gold and pure silver was issued. In the introduction of this new currency, however, a wise regard seems to have been had to the weight of the previously current electrum staters, each of which was thenceforth to be represented by an equal value, though of course not by an equal weight of pure gold. Thus the old Græco-Asiatic electrum stater of 220 grains was replaced by a new pure gold stater of 168 grains, equivalent, like

[1] Herod. i. 46, 50, 92.   [2] Hist. Gr. Eng. Tr. vol. ii. p. 115.

its predecessor in electrum, to 10 silver staters of 220 grains (one-fifth of the Græco-Asiatic silver mina), as current in the coast towns; and the old Babylonic electrum stater of 168 grains was replaced by a new pure gold stater of 126 grains, equal in value, like it, to one-fifth of the Babylonic silver mina, or to 10 silver staters of 168 grains as now for the first time coined. This latter gold stater possessed moreover the advantage of being also equivalent to one-half of the Phocaic gold stater of 256 grains (maximum), a coin which therefore, very soon after its introduction, became superfluous in the Lydian currency. The κροίσειος στατήρ, weighing 126 grains, was therefore equally acceptable, both in the East, where the Babylonian system was universal, and in the West, wherever the Phocaic system had been adopted. Hence the gold pieces of 126 grains were coined in far larger quantities than the heavier pieces of 168 grains, the circulation of which was of a more limited and local character.

Each of these gold staters was divided, according to the ancient Asiatic system, into thirds, sixths, and twelfths, so that there were no less than eight different denominations of gold money issued simultaneously by Crœsus when he reformed the Lydian coinage, one and all bearing the arms of the Imperial city Sardes, the fore-parts of the Lion and the Bull facing each other.

The silver stater, which Crœsus introduced for the first time into Lydia, was so regulated as to stand in the fixed legal proportion of ten to one gold stater of 126 grains. Not that Crœsus was the first to introduce this decimal system, for it had existed in the earlier times, not only in Lydia, but in Babylon, for uncoined gold and silver: the Babylonian silver mina having been constituted of a weight, which at the fixed proportionate value of 13·3 to 1, should exchange for $\frac{1}{10}$ of the gold mina. The manifest convenience of exchange thus secured was, there can be no doubt, the reason why the weights of the silver talent, mina, and shekel were regulated in such a manner that 10 talents, 10 minæ, or 10 shekels of silver should be the recognized price of 1 talent, 1 mina, or 1 shekel of gold. But Crœsus was the first to apply to *coined* silver the ancient Babylonic system; his silver stater of 168 grains being the 50th part of the light Babylonian silver mina, just as his gold stater of 126 grains was the 50th part of the light Babylonian gold mina.

The silver money of Crœsus bore uniformly the same type as the gold, and was divided into halves, thirds and twelfths, weighing respectively 84, 56, and 14 grains. What is especially noticeable in this coinage is the multiplicity of the denominations and the fixity and uniformity of type. This is in fact the earliest Imperial coinage in the history of the world, and to Crœsus must be ascribed the initiation of a currency on a comprehensive scale as distinguished from the more or less local and circumscribed issues of other contemporary States; a currency which was doubtless designed by him to supersede all existing mintages, and to be accepted throughout Asia Minor as the sole Imperial coinage. The object of Crœsus seems to have been to give his Lydian money an international character; hence the extreme care taken that the weight of every denomination should be so fixed and determined as to represent exactly the value of some one or other of the many municipal and local coins current at the time, not only in his own dominions, but in independent Greek cities.

That this grand attempt to inaugurate a universal currency failed to attain a lasting success is due, not so much to any inherent impracticability in a design which would have been at that time, in a far higher measure than in the present day, a real boon to mankind at large, and a material aid and advancement of future civilizing influences; but its failure was due to events which Crœsus could not foresee, and which, could he have foreseen them, he would have been powerless to ward off.

The following Table may serve to exhibit to the reader the whole system of the Lydian currency as reformed by Crœsus, with all its ingenious and elaborate combinations:—

LYDIA. TIME OF CRŒSUS, B.C. 568–554.

GOLD OF LYDIA.　　　　EQUIVALENTS IN NATIVE AND FOREIGN MONEY OF THE TIME.

	IN GOLD.	IN ELECTRUM.	IN SILVER.
(i) BABYLONIC SILVER STANDARD.			
N Stater [Pl. I. 9]　168 grs. =		1 Grœco-As. stater . . 224 grs.	10 Grœco-Asiatic staters of 224 grs. 20　 ,,　　 $\frac{1}{2}$　 ,,　 112 ,, 40　 ,,　　 $\frac{1}{4}$　 ,,　 56 ,,
N Trite . . . . . 56 grs. =		1　 ,,　　 ,, trite . . . 74 ,,	6 Euboic staters of 124 grs. 12　 ,,　 drachms of 62 grs.
N Hecte . . . . 28 grs. =		1　 ,,　　 ,, hecte　　 37　 ,,	6　 ,,　　 ,, of 62 ,,
N Hemihecton . . 14 grs. =		1　 ,,　　 ,, hemihecton 18　 ,,	3　 ,,　　 ,, of 62 ,,
(ii) EUBOIC STANDARD.			
N Stater [Pl. I. 10]　126 grs. =	$\frac{1}{2}$ Phocaic stater of 253 grs.	1 Babylonic stater of 168　 ,,	10 Babylonic staters of 168 grs. 20　 ,,　 drachms of 84 grs. 30 Grœco-Asiatic $\frac{1}{2}$ staters of 56 grs. 40 Euboic tetrobols of 42 grs.
N Trite [Pl. I. 11]　42 grs. =	1 N Phocaic hecte of 42 grs. . . .		10 Grœco-Asiatic $\frac{1}{2}$ staters of 56 grs.
N Hecte . . . . . 21 grs. =	1 N　 ,,　 hemihecton of 21 grs.		10 { Grœco-As. trihemiobols Babylonic diobols } of 28 grs.
N Hemihecton . . . 11 grs. =	1 N　 ,,　 twenty-fourth, 11 grs.		10 Babylonic obols of 14 grs.

SILVER OF LYDIA.　　　　　EQUIVALENT IN LYDIAN GOLD.

BABYLONIC STANDARD.		
R Stater [Pl. I. 12]　168 grs. =	$\frac{1}{15}$ of the gold stater of 126 grs.	
R $\frac{1}{2}$ Stater [Pl. I. 13]　84 grs. =	$\frac{1}{30}$　 ,,　　 ,,　　 ,, 126 grs.	
R $\frac{1}{4}$ Stater . . . . 56 grs. =	$\frac{1}{45}$　 ,,　　 ,,　　 ,, 126 grs,	
R $\frac{1}{12}$ Stater . . . 14 grs. =	$\frac{1}{180}$　 ,,　　 ,,　　 ,, 126 grs. or $\frac{1}{12}$ of the N Hemihecton of 11 grs.	

N.B.—In the above Tables fractions of grains are not given.

SOUTH FRONT OF THE PALACE OF DARIUS, PERSEPOLIS, RESTORED (AFTER FLANDIN).

PART II.

PERSIA.

The events which led to the downfall of Crœsus from the height of his prosperity and power, and to the incorporation of his dominions, including the Greek coast towns, into the Empire of Cyrus, are too well known to need repetition here. This is commonly supposed to have occurred in the year B.C. 546, but the latest investigations point to the year 554 as the most probable date. But, however momentous the change from a political point of view, nevertheless it is almost certain that no immediate alteration in the coinage was attempted by the new rulers of Western Asia: for it must be remembered that the Persians, like the Medes and Babylonians, were at this time without a specific coinage of their own; the tradition which ascribes the origin of the daric to a King of Persia of the name of Darius, who is said to have been one of the predecessors of Cyrus, being unworthy of credit, as it rests only upon the statement of Harpocration.[1]

The electrum coinage of the Greek cities had already been superseded by the Imperial

[1] s.v. Δαρεικός—οὐχ ὡς οἱ πλεῖστοι νομίζουσιν, ἀπὸ Δαρείου τοῦ Ξέρξου πατρός, ἀλλ᾽ ἀφ᾽ ἑτέρου τινὸς παλαιοτέρου βασιλέως. As Harpocration was an Alexandrian Greek, who lived certainly not earlier than the second century A.D., no value whatever should be attached to a statement of this sort. The whole passage in which it occurs was copied at a later period by Suidas, and again inserted by Musurus in the Aldine edition of the Scholiasts ad Aristoph. Eccles., 602.

Perhaps Xenophon is responsible for the error of Harpocration; for in his Cyropædeia (v. 2, 7) he represents darics as in use in the time of Cyrus I.: ἐπειδὴ δὲ ἔνδον ἦσαν ἐωράων ὁ Γωβρύας φιάλας χρυσᾶς καὶ πρόχους καὶ κάλπιδας καὶ κόσμον παντοῖον καὶ δαρεικοὺς ἀμέτρους τινὰς καὶ πάντα καλά, καὶ τέλος τὴν θυγατέρα κ.τ.λ. It is needless to say that this work of Xenophon's is a mere romance, and utterly without historical value.

currency of Lydia; and, in the times of distress and impoverishment which followed the Persian conquest, it is unreasonable to suppose that there could have been any revived mintage in those towns with the single exception of Samos, which, under the rule of Polycrates, still maintained its independence until B.C. 520.

Whether or not the Persian Governor of Sardes continued to issue the gold and silver money of Crœsus during the reigns of Cyrus and Cambyses must remain, for the present, a matter for conjecture. It is possible, and even probable, if we may judge from the quantities of these coins which have escaped the Persian melting-pot, that no change was at first made in the arrangements of the Sardian mint, and that both gold and silver money was put into circulation from time to time as necessity required, the old dies being retained, as a matter of course; for it was not part of the policy of Cyrus to introduce uncalled-for changes in the internal government of the various conquered States which contributed to form the vast Empire of Persia. The blending of the motley throng into one homogeneous whole was reserved for the organizing spirit of Darius, the son of Hystaspes, in whose reign the famous Persian "Archers" first went forth into the world.

PERSIAN SUBJECTS BRINGING TRIBUTE TO THE KING (PERSEPOLIS).

The first five years of the reign of Darius were occupied in the extinction of a series of formidable rebellions in various parts of his extensive dominions, and it was not till the year B.C. 516 that he found leisure to devote his mind to the civil organization of his Empire. The division of the whole into Satrapies, at first twenty in number, and the imposition upon each of these principalities of a fixed sum of money to be collected by the several Satraps, and to be paid by them into the royal treasury, was one of the methods which Darius adopted for welding into one coherent State, the various Provinces which together constituted the Persian Empire. The assessment of this tribute led to the institution of an Imperial coinage, the first idea of which may have been suggested to Darius by the gold and silver money of Lydia still circulating in the western Satrapies since the time of Crœsus. It is probable also that the manifest advantages of current money, guaranteed by the State, were beginning to be appreciated beyond the limits of Asia Minor, to which it had hitherto been confined; and the system of rapid communication, by means of post horses and couriers, between the most distant portions of the empire and the capital, would naturally tend in no small degree to facilitate the adoption of the Western habit of receiving and paying sums of gold and silver by tale, without having recourse to weights and scales, as had been hitherto the custom in the East.

An Imperial coinage once decided upon, the first and most important consideration for the Great King was necessarily the standard which would be most easily understood by his subjects, and in the choice of this there could not have been room for much hesitation; for, with the exception of Syria, Phœnicia, and the Greek coast towns, where the so-called Græco-Asiatic or Phœnician standard prevailed, the Babylonian gold and silver talents were everywhere in use. Darius had therefore only to follow in the footsteps of Crœsus, by whom the Babylonian standard had already been adopted.

Nevertheless the Persian Imperial coinage differed considerably from that of Lydia, and was as simple as the latter was complex. We have seen that in the Lydian coinage of Crœsus there were no less than eight different denominations of gold money, each of which was regulated in such a manner as to pass readily at a fixed equivalent in the markets of the tributary Greek towns in exchange for the local electrum and silver money of the district, of whatever standard that might happen to be, as may be seen by referring to the table given above (p. 21). Darius could afford to cast all such considerations to the winds. The very extent of his enormous Empire rendered any attempt at following out the minute arrangements of the Lydian royal coinage impracticable. Simplicity therefore is the chief characteristic of the Persian Imperial currency as first determined by Darius. There was to be one denomination of gold and one of silver, the gold piece to be worth 20 pieces of silver. This result might doubtless have been arrived at without issuing a new coinage, by simply retaining the gold stater of Crœsus of 126 grs., and the silver drachm or siglos of 84 grs., and allowing all the other denominations of the intricate Lydian system to fall into disuse: but the type of the Lydian coin, the Lion and the Bull, was hardly appropriate to the money of the Great King, and if, as may well have been the case, this type possessed any symbolic or religious signification, it would moreover have been repugnant to the prejudices of an earnest Zoroastrian like Darius. The image of the Great King himself was accordingly substituted for the Lion and Bull—this one type, which I shall describe more minutely later on, being adopted for the Royal coins of both metals.

Darius, although he selected the gold stater of Crœsus of 126 grs., and his siglos of

84 grs., as the prototypes of the Persian currency, sought nevertheless to give his new money a prestige of its own, by making a small addition to the weight both of the gold and of the silver coin. These seem to have been fixed respectively at 130 and 86 grs. In this, perhaps, the normal weights of the Babylonian gold and silver talents may have been reverted to, which in their passage westwards and during the lapse of time may be supposed to have suffered some slight diminution.

The metal of the Persian money, especially of the gold coinage, was of remarkable purity, —the daric, according to an analysis furnished by Letronne (Considérations, p. 108), containing only 3 per cent. of alloy. The result was, that the Persian gold coinage immediately obtained a reputation which enabled it to supersede the gold money of all other states, and to maintain its position as the sole gold currency in the ancient world. As long as and wherever Persia was supreme, the coinage of gold remained a prerogative of the Great King.

Not so the silver currency: for the very fact of the siglos being the only Imperial silver piece is sufficient to prove that it could never have been intended to supersede the many smaller and larger denominations necessary for small traffic and retail trade actually current in many districts of the Empire. The silver coinage was not the sole prerogative of the Great King or even of the Satraps, but appears to have been issued by the Great King, by his Satraps, and by large numbers of subject or tributary towns, according to their various requirements.

The coinage of the Persian Empire may be divided into four main categories:—

I. THE ROYAL COINAGE.

II. THE PROVINCIAL COINS WITH ROYAL TYPES.

III. THE SATRAPAL COINAGE.

IV. THE LOCAL COINAGES OF THE TRIBUTARY STATES.

In the following pages I propose to consider the first two of the above classes only. A separate article in the Numismata Orientalia by Prof. Julius Euting, of Strassburg, is, I understand, to be devoted to the coins with Phœnician and Aramaic inscriptions, among which those of the Satraps will be included. The local coinages of the Greek tributary cities, although these undoubtedly formed part of the Persian Empire, we may dismiss as beyond the scope of the Numismata Orientalia.

I. THE ROYAL COINAGE.

Of the Royal Persian Coinage, commencing with Darius, the son of Hystaspes, and ending with the Macedonian conquest, the following varieties are known. The uniformity of style and the absence of inscriptions renders it impossible to classify them according to the several reigns in which they must have been issued.

GOLD.

Darics.

WEIGHT.	OBVERSE.	REVERSE.
129·7	The king, bearded, crowned, and clad in the Persian *candys*, kneeling r. on one knee, at his back a quiver, in his right a spear, and in his outstretched l. a strung bow. [Brit. Mus. Plate I. 14.]	Irregular incuse of oblong form.
128·7	Similar, of more recent style. [Brit. Mus. Plate I. 15.]	Similar.
127·5	The king, bearded, crowned, and clad in long robe, with belt round waist, and annulets or buttons in front, kneeling r. on one knee; at his back a quiver, in his r. an arrow, and in his outstretched l. a strung bow. [Brit. Mus. Plate I. 16.]	Similar.
132	Youthful king, without beard, wearing on his head the *kidaris*, and clad in long robe, close-fitting and flecked, with sleeves to the elbow and trousers to the knee of the same material. He kneels r. on one knee, and holds spear in r. and strung bow in outstretched l. [Mus. Luynes, 132 grs., Brit. Mus. 126·8 grs.] [Plate I. 17.]	Irregular oblong incuse, containing a naked figure seated, with arm raised above head; beside the incuse a countermark? also incuse, representing a bearded head of Pan having stag's horns. The figure within the incuse, as well as the little head of Pan, are of Greek work.

Double Darics.

258	The king, bearded, crowned, and clad in Persian *candys*, kneeling r. on one knee, at his back a quiver, in his r. spear, and in l. strung bow: no letters or symbols. [Coll. de Luynes.]	Irregular incuse, crossed by wavy lines in relief.

Seven or eight specimens of the double daric, as above described, without letters or symbols in the field, have been published at various times. One of them was found in 1826 near Philadelphia in Lydia. See Madden, Jewish Coinage, p. 273.

WEIGHT.	OBVERSE.		REVERSE.
257·5	Similar. In field, l. wreath; r. M.	Similar.	
	[Bank of England. Plate I. 18.]		
257	Similar ?	Similar.	
	[Cabinet of M. Six.]		
257	Similar. In field, l. wreath; r. X or X.	Similar.	
	[Cabinet de France. Plate I. 19.]		
257	Similar. In field, l. A.	Similar.	
	[Imhoof-Blumer. Plate I. 20.]		
?	Similar. In field, l. ΛY.	Similar.	
	[Zeitschrift. f. Num. Bd. iii. p. 351.]		
254·5	Similar. In field, wreath.	Similar.	
	[Cabinet de France. Plate I. 21.]		
256	Similar. In field, tiara with band ?	Similar.	
	[Ivanoff 665.]		
257	Similar. In field, l. Φl.	Similar.	
	[Cabinet de France. Another at the Hague. Plate I. 22.]		
255	Similar. In field, l. ♌.	Similar.	
	[Cabinet de France. Plate I. 23.]		
255	Similar. In field, l. ⅄.	Similar.	
	[Cat. Hoffmann, Feb. 1874. Plate I. 24.]		
252	Similar. In field, l. ℞.	Incuse square irregularly divided.	
	[Coll. de Vogüé.]		

SILVER.

Sigli.

83·7	The king, bearded, crowned, and clad in the Persian *candys*, kneeling r. on one knee, at his back a quiver, in his r. a spear, and in his outstretched l. a strung bow.	Irregular incuse of oblong form.	
	[Brit. Mus. Plate I. 25.]		

Weight.	Obverse.	Obverse.
85	The king, bearded, crowned, and clad in long robe, with belt round waist, and ornamented with annulets or buttons in front, kneeling r. on one knee, at his back a quiver, in his r. an arrow, and in his outstretched l. a strung bow. [Brit. Mus. Plate I. 26.]	Similar.
84·7	Similar, but king holds short sword or dagger instead of arrow. [Brit. Mus. Plate I. 27.]	Similar.
83·4	The king, bearded, crowned, and clad in Persian *candys*, kneeling r. on one knee and drawing bow; at his back quiver. [Brit. Mus. Plate I. 28.]	Similar.
82·6	The king, half length, bearded, crowned, and clad in Persian *candys*. He holds short sword in his r. and strung bow in his l. [Brit. Mus. Plate I. 29.]	Similar.

A close examination of the gold darics enables us to perceive that, in spite of their general similarity, there are differences of style. Some are archaic, and date from the time of Darius and Xerxes, while others are characterized by more careful work, and those belong to the later monarchs of the Achœmenian dynasty.[1]

Among those latter are to be classed the double darics, of which about twenty specimens have been published at various times. The double darics, however, are not purely Persian, but bear evidence of having been struck in Greek cities, as the greater number of the known specimens have Greek letters or symbols in the field. The same remark applies to the daric (No. 4) with a portrait of a youthful king, and with a bearded head of Pan of Greek work incuse on the reverse, a symbol which may, however, be a countermark. It is not an easy matter to affirm with certainty to what district of Asia Minor the double darics ought to be assigned; but a comparison of their style with that of the silver staters figured in Pl. III. 14–20 leads me to infer that they were struck in the western portion of Asia Minor.

Herodotus (iv. 166) is the first Greek writer who alludes to the gold money of Darius, who he said was "anxious to leave such a memorial of himself as had been accomplished by no other king;" wherefore, "having refined gold to the utmost perfection, he struck money."

As early as the time of the expedition of Xerxes against Greece, immense numbers of these gold coins must have been in circulation, for the Lydian Pythius had in his own

---

[1] Lenormant's attempt to attribute the darics to the several reigns according to the differences in the portraits of the king as visible upon them appears to me to be a refinement of classification.

possession as many as 3,993,000 of them, a sum which Xerxes, by presenting him with 7000 in addition, was munificent enough to make up to the good round total of four million.[1]

It is remarkable that no writer mentions the double daric; hence we may infer that the issue of these coins was restricted probably to a single district, and that they were not minted during any long period of time.

Half-darics are by some supposed to be alluded to by Xenophon in the following passage: προσαιτοῦσι δὲ μισθὸν ὁ Κῦρος ὑπισχνεῖται ἡμιόλιον πᾶσι δώσειν οὐ πρότερον ἔφερον ἀντὶ δαρεικοῦ τρία ἡμιδαρεικὰ τοῦ μηνὸς τῷ στρατιώτῃ (Anab. i. 3, 21). None of these coins have been handed down to us, nor do I see that we are bound to take Xenophon's words, ἀντὶ δαρεικοῦ τρία ἡμιδαρεικά, to mean literally that each soldier had three golden half-darics promised him every month. I should rather be inclined to take τρία ἡμιδαρεικὰ simply to mean a sum of money equivalent to a daric and a half (cf. τριημι——, the ordinary way of expressing one and a half).

The royal silver coin is in every respect similar to the daric, and may even sometimes have been called by the same name,[2] but the ordinary appellation appears to have been the σίγλος Μηδικός, or simply σίγλος. Xenophon (Anab. i. 5, 6) furnishes us with a most valuable datum as to the current value of the σίγλος in Attic money, "ὁ δὲ σίγλος δύναται ἑπτὰ ὀβολοὺς καὶ ἡμιωβόλιον Αττικούς." This gives us a weight of 84·37 English grains, which is the full average weight of the sigli that have come down to us. The type of the σίγλος is not so constant as that of the daric, and many specimens betray great carelessness of workmanship.

The normal weight of the Persian silver must be placed as high as 86·45 grs., although the average actual weight is only about that given by Xenophon. The siglos was the half of the Perso-Babylonic silver stater of 172·9 grs. so frequently met with in the towns along the south coast of Asia Minor, in Crete and in Cyprus, etc. Consequently it may be correctly designated as a drachm (the term *drachm* being properly applicable only to the half-stater), one hundred of which constituted a Perso-Babylonic silver mina of 8645 grs., and 6000 the talent.

Having thus ascertained the weight of the Persian drachm, it remains to be seen how many of these coins exchanged for one daric. Here again Xenophon comes to our assistance, and supplies us, though indirectly, with the required information in the following passage: ἐνταῦθα Κῦρος Σιλανὸν καλέσας τὸν Ἀμπρακιώτην μάντιν ἔδωκεν αὐτῷ δαρεικοὺς τρισχιλίους, ὅτι τῇ ἑνδεκάτῃ ἀπ᾽ ἐκείνης τῆς ἡμέρας πρότερον θυόμενος εἶπεν αὐτῷ ὅτι βασιλεὺς οὐ μαχεῖται δέκα ἡμερῶν Κῦρος δ᾽ εἶπεν. Οὐκ ἄρα ἔτι μαχεῖται, εἰ ἐν ταύταις οὐ μαχεῖται ταῖς ἡμέραις· ἐὰν δ᾽ ἀληθεύσῃς, ὑπισχνοῦμαί σοι δέκα τάλαντα. Τοῦτο τὸ χρυσίον τότε ἀπέδωκεν ἐπεὶ παρῆλθον αἱ δέκα ἡμέραι (Anab. i. 7, 18). Whence it follows that 300 gold darics were considered by Cyrus the Younger as equal to 1 talent, or, in other words, to 6000 sigli. Hence 5 darics would be worth 1 mina, and 1 daric would be current for 20 sigli. We also see from the

[1] Herod. vii. 28.

[2] Plutarch, Cimon x. 11, Λέγεται γέ τοι Ῥοισάκην τινὰ βάρβαρον ἀποστάτην βασιλέως ἐλθεῖν μετὰ χρημάτων πολλῶν εἰς Ἀθήνας καὶ συκοφαντούμενον ὑπὸ τῶν συκοφαντῶν καταφυγεῖν πρὸς Κίμωνα, καὶ θεῖναι παρὰ τὴν αὔλειον αὐτοῦ φιάλας δύο, τὴν μὲν ἀργυρείων, ἐμπλησάμενον Δαρεικῶν, τὴν δὲ χρυσῶν.

above calculation that the relative value of gold to silver in Asia 'was still as 13·3 : 1, hence:

$$1 \; N \text{ Daric of 130 grs. } \times 13·3 = 1729 \text{ grs. of silver} = \begin{cases} 10 \text{ Perso-Babylonic staters of } 172·9 \\ 20 \text{ Sigli } \; . \; . \; . \; . \; . \text{ of } 86·45 \\ 15 \text{ Phœnician drachms } \; . \text{ of } \; 115 \\ 30 \quad ,, \qquad \text{drachms } \; . \text{ of } \quad 57 \end{cases}$$

It is the *Persian* therefore, and not the *Attic* drachm, which we must understand when Harpocration, in his Lexicon, s.v. Daricus, says, λέγουσι δέ τινες δύνασθαι τὸν Δαρεικὸν ἀργυρᾶς δραχμὰς κ, ὡς τοὺς ἑ Δαρεικοὺς δίνασθαι μνᾶν ἀργυρίου.

i.e. 1 Daric=20 [Persian] silver drachms.
5 Darics=1 [Perso-Babylonic] silver mina.

There is absolutely no evidence in favour of the opinion which has been advanced by some, that the daric was worth 20 *Attic* drachms, for even in Greece, where gold was cheaper than in Asia, it must have been worth at least 24 Attic drachms, and in all probability passed current for 25, while in Asia it was worth more than 25½, the relative value of coined gold to coined silver in European Greece having been until the time of Philip of Macedon, and according to Brandis (p. 251) even later, as high as 12½ : 1.

Naturally a single silver coin like the Persian drachm could not suffice for the wants of the people, and it was probably at no time the intention of the Great King to supersede the local silver coinages, although the royal money was perhaps the only legally recognized currency, and the only coin accepted by the government at its nominal or current value, all other moneys being simply received by weight, and afterwards melted down and preserved in the royal treasury as bullion until the time came to coin them again into darics and sigli, when just so much and no more than was necessary for the immediate need was put into circulation.[1]

The capital punishment inflicted by Darius upon Aryandes, the Satrap of Egypt, must not be taken as evidence that the Great King reserved for himself the sole prerogative of striking silver as well as gold, for Aryandes was not punished with death for coining silver, but for coining it of finer quality than the money of the Great King; and even this offence was not considered sufficient to warrant his execution, for Darius had to bring another charge against him, viz. that he was planning a rebellion, before he felt himself authorized to order him to be put to death.[2]

[1] Brandis, p. 219. Herod. iii. 89, 96.

ἀρχὰς δὲ καὶ φόρων πρόσοδον τὴν ἐπέτειον κατὰ τάδε διεῖλε. τοῖσι μὲν αὐτέων ἀργύριον ἀπαγινούσι, εἴρητο Βαβυλώνιον σταθμὸν τάλαντον ἀπαγινέειν· τοῖσι δὲ χρυσίον ἀπαγινούσι, Εὐβοϊκόν. τὸ δὲ Βαβυλώνιον τάλαντον δύναται Εὐβοΐδας ἑβδομήκοντα μνέας. (iii. 89.)

τοῦτον τὸν φόρον θησαυρίζει· ὁ βασιλεὺς τρόπῳ τοιῷδε. ἐς πίθους κεραμίνους τήξας καταχέει· πλήσας δὲ τὸ ἄγγος, περιαιρέει τὸν κέραμον. ἐπεὰν δὲ δεηθῇ χρημάτων, κατακόπτει τοσοῦτο ὅσου ἂν ἑκάστοτε δέηται. (iii. 96.)

In the first of these passages, and in the calculations which follow it, errors have crept into the text. It has been proved by Mommsen (ed. Dietz, vol. i. p. 28) that instead of 70 Euboic minæ being equal in weight to one Babylonic talent, Herodotus must have written 78. See also Brandis, p. 63, sq.

[2] Herod. iv. 166 : ὁ δὲ Ἀρυάνδης . . . . ἰδὼν Δαρεῖον ἐπιθυμέοντα μνημόσυνον ἑωυτοῦ λιπέσθαι, τοῦτο τὸ μὴ ἄλλῳ οἴη βασιλέϊ κατιργασμένον, ἐμιμέετο τοῦτον· ἐς οὗ ἔλαβε τὸν μισθόν. Δαρεῖος μὲν γὰρ χρυσίον καθαρώτατον ἀπεψήσας ἐς τὸ δυνατώτατον, νόμισμα ἐκόψατο· Ἀρυάνδης δὲ, ἄρχων Αἰγύπτου, ἀργύριον τὼυτὸ τοῦτο ἐποίεε· καὶ νῦν ἐστι ἀργύριον καθαρώτατον τὸ Ἀρυανδικόν. μαθὼν δὲ Δαρεῖός μιν ταῦτα ποιεῦντα, αἰτίην οἱ ἄλλην ἐπενείκας, ὅτι οἱ ἐπανιστέαιτο, ἀπέκτεινε. This silver money was still circulating in the time of Herodotus, but no specimens are now known, for Brandis has restored to Phœnicia (Kings of Byblos) the coins formerly attributed to Aryandes by Ch. Lenormant. The inscription ΑΡΤΑΝ, said by some to be legible on one or more of these coins, is not sufficiently distinct to warrant us in transferring to Aryandes a series of coins so manifestly Phœnician in character as the pieces alluded to.

II. THE PROVINCIAL COINS WITH ROYAL TYPES.

PERSIAN KING HUNTING THE LION, FROM THE SIGNET-CYLINDER OF DARIUS-HYSTASPIS.

Under this head I propose to include several distinct series of coins, which, however, have this in common, viz. that they all bear evidence of having been issued under the auspices of the Great King. On some he will be seen in his chariot accompanied by his charioteer and engaged in the favourite royal pastime of the chase; on others also in his chariot, but in stately procession, and followed by an attendant, who holds over him a standard or sceptre; on others, contending with a rampant lion, which he seizes by the mane, and is about to stab with a short sword; while on others again we shall see him, as on the Imperial coinage, as a kneeling archer. On another, and a distinct series, his portrait only will appear wearing the tiara, and sometimes the word $Βασιλεύς$, accompanying some merely local type, will sufficiently prove that the coin was issued by some city subject to the authority of the King.

KING CONTENDING WITH A LION (PERSEPOLIS).

It will not be always possible to say in what locality, or under whose reign, these various coins were struck; but that they were current in different districts of the Persian Empire in the time of the successors of Darius there can be no room for doubt. Neither can it be a matter for dispute that these several currencies are provincial or local in character rather than Imperial, for the weight-systems according to which they are regulated enable us to define within certain limits the districts of the empire in which they must have circulated.

Of these districts the most important is that which lay between the Euphrates and the Phœnician sea, which formed part of the Ninth and Fifth Satrapies of the Empire. In the interior of this district were situated the important cities of Thapsacus on the Tigris, the residence of the Satrap of Syria, of Bambyce, of Chalybon, of Hamath, and of Damascus, where was a royal treasury; while on the coast were the far-famed Phœnician towns of Sidon, of Tyro, of

Byblus, of Arndus, of Marathus, and others. Those latter, for the most part governed by their own kings, struck also their own coins, municipal or regal, which may, for convenience sake, be distinguished from those which bear Persian types, and which I shall not include in the present article. Whether the Phœnician cities on the sea-coast, or the Syrian towns on the upper reaches of the Euphrates, are the places where the coins which I am about to include in Series I. and II. were minted, it is difficult to determine with certainty. The weight-system of this currency is identical with that which is prevalent on the Phœnician coast at the cities of Tyre, Byblus, and Arudus; while the fact that specimens of these coins have been found in the Tigris is no proof of a Syrian origin, and perhaps only indicates the course of the Phœnician trade with the interior, and shows that the Phœnician system of weights and money extended from the Tigris and the Euphrates to the sea.

It will be seen from the description which follows how much these pieces have in common with the recognized money of Phœnicia both in type and fabric. Indeed, were it not that the forms of some of the letters upon a few of the inscribed specimens seem to be of an Aramaic rather than a purely Phœnician character, all the evidence would be in favour of the coins which follow being Perso-Phœnician rather than Perso-Syrian.

PHŒNICIAN DIRHME (KOUYUNJIK).

SERIES I.

CLASS 1.

PHŒNICIAN STANDARD.

Double Shekel or Octadrachm.

WEIGHT.	OBVERSE.	REVERSE.
422·8	Phœnician war-galley, with mast, sails, and oars advancing l., beneath, waves; the whole within a border of dots.	Incuse square, within which the king accompanied by charioteer in quadriga l., the horses walking. In the upper portion of the square is the fore-part of a wild goat standing towards l. with head looking r., the goat incuse.

[Brit. Mus. Plate II. 1.]

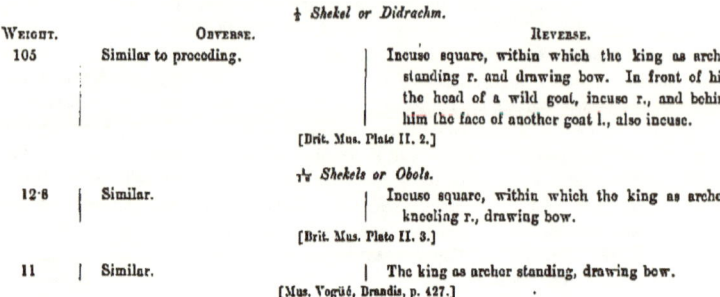

⅓ Shekel or Didrachm.

WEIGHT.	OBVERSE.	REVERSE.
105	Similar to preceding.	Incuse square, within which the king as archer standing r. and drawing bow. In front of him the head of a wild goat, incuse r., and behind him the face of another goat l., also incuse.

[Brit. Mus. Plate II. 2.]

¹⁄₁₂ Shekels or Obols.

12·8	Similar.	Incuse square, within which the king as archer, kneeling r., drawing bow.

[Brit. Mus. Plate II. 3.]

11	Similar.	The king as archer standing, drawing bow.

[Mus. Vogüé, Brandis, p. 427.]

These four coins are remarkable as furnishing us with a representation of a war-galley under sail, a type which points clearly to Phœnicia, for on the Tigris and Euphrates ships of this description with sails were never used. The reverse types, on the other hand, are clearly Persian, and the union of the two seems to indicate that this class of coins was issued for the convenience of the traders between the interior and the coast. The place of mintage may therefore have been Tyre, whose close commercial relations with Syria and with the interior of Asia generally are well known, cf. Ezekiel, xxvii., who, in his picture of the glory of Tyre, says, "Syria was thy dealer from the multitude of thy fabrics: with jewels and purple and embroidery and cotton and corals and rubies they furnished thy markets. . . . . . Damascus was thy dealer in the multitude of thy fabrics from the abundance of all riches, in the wine of Helbon (Χαλυβών, Aleppo) and white wool."

The obverse type of these coins would seem, as is not unfrequently the case in the archaic period, to be the one which indicates the place of issue. The Persian reverse in the present instance is perhaps only intended as an assertion of the supremacy of the Great King, and as a sort of guarantee that the coins should pass current in the interior as well as in Phœnicia. The two types taken in this sense as having a double reference to the actual place of mintage, governed by its own semi-independent rulers, and to the lands under the direct government of the Great King, may be compared with the double inscriptions on the Lion weights of an earlier age in Cuneiform and in Phœnician characters: "Fifteen manehs of the King—fifteen manehs of the country. Five manehs of the King—five manehs of the country," etc. etc.

Of the cities of Phœnicia, Tyre is one to which, in my opinion, the type of the obverse seems to point with especial appropriateness. Ezekiel (chapter xxvii.) had already likened this city, seated in the midst of the waters, to a ship. "Thy borders are in the heart of the waters; thy builders have perfected thy beauty. They have made all thy planks of fir from Shenir; they have taken cedar from Lebanon to make thee a mast. Of the oaks of

Bashan they have made thine oars; thy row-benches of ivory in box from the coasts of Chittim. Fine linen with embroidery from Egypt was spread out for thy sail; thine awning was of blue and purple from the coasts of Greece. The inhabitants of Zidon and Arvad were thy mariners. Thy skilful men, O Tyre, were in thee as pilots," etc. etc.[1]

The large size of some of these coins is also an indication of their having been minted by some city of great commercial renown, such as Tyre, which was at one time pre-eminent among all the cities of the Persian Empire in this respect, although the claims of Sidon ought not to be overlooked.

The types of the reverses of the coins above described, although most distinctly Persian in character, betray nevertheless a peculiarity of workmanship which would seem to have been not unusual in Phœnicia. I allude to the strange habit of making an incuse addition to the type in the shape of an animal, which is sometimes a symbol, as on these coins, and sometimes forms an integral part of the type, as on the coins of some of the Kings of Byblus (see Brandis, pp. 511–12). This incuse addition must not be mistaken for a countermark. In the present instances the fore-part of the ibex or wild goat is added to the main type on the octadrachm, perhaps to convey the idea that it is the ibex which the Great King is represented as setting out in his chariot to hunt. This animal is enumerated among others as frequently hunted by the early Assyrian kings in the region of the Upper Tigris and in Syria (Rawlinson, Anc. Mon., 1st ed. vol. i. p. 279). It is also mentioned by Xenophon (Cyrop. i. 47) as one of the animals hunted by Cyrus.

---

[1] The translation as given above is from Mr. Kenrick's Phœnicia, p. 193.

PERSIAN KING KILLING WILD GOAT (FROM A CYLINDER).

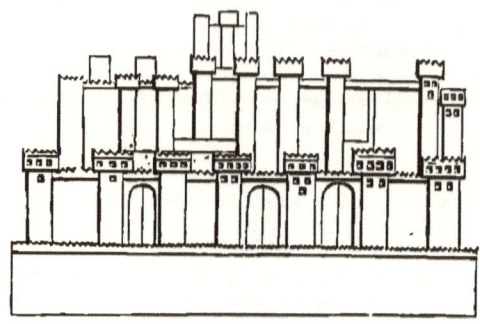

FORTIFIED PLACE BELONGING TO AN ENEMY OF THE ASSYRIANS (NIMRUD).

CLASS 2.

PHŒNICIAN STANDARD.

Double Shekels or Octadrachms.

WEIGHT.	OBVERSE.	REVERSE.
425	City-wall with five battlemented towers, before which lies an armed galley. At the stern is a standard, surmounted by a disc and crescent. In the exergue are two lions back to back. Above the exergual line the Phœnician letters ʃO . . . cable border.	Incuse circle and dotted border, within which the king and his charioteer in quadriga, l.; horses galloping; beneath the horses an ibex or wild goat, *incuse*, stretched out towards l., its head turned right. Under the goat a Phœnician inscription (retrograde?) OႱႡ⅍?

[Brit. Mus. Plate II. 4.]

414·5	Similar. (To right of wall a man standing.) No inscription.	Similar, (man behind chariot,) beneath . . ႱჃO ?

[Brit. Mus. Plate II. 5.]

426	Similar.	Similar, but border within circle plain. No inscription, and no figure behind chariot.

[Brit. Mus. Plate II. 6, reverse only engraved.]

416·2	Similar.	Similar, border dotted. Above chariot in field, l. the Phœnician letters Oႄ.

[Brit. Mus., much worn.]

The above described pieces are all in the British Museum. Nos. 2 and 3 are said to
have been found in the Tigris in the year 1818. They were originally in the collection of
Mr. Rich. I give the Phœnician letters as I see them. Though very indistinct, they are
certainly Phœnician characters, and in no case Greek. This leads me to infer that the letters
on a similar coin in the Behr Collection (No. 839), which M. F. Lenormant read AYPA,
and explained as the beginning of the name Aryandes, retrograde, are probably also Phœnician,
and that they have been misread by Lenormant; for Brandis, on the same coin, failed to
decipher the letters AYPA.

With the reverse type may be compared the signet cylinder of Darius, the son of Hystaspes,
now in the British Museum (engraved above, p. 31), representing the King with his charioteer
hunting the lion. The action of the horses and the position of the dead lion beneath them,
bear so striking a resemblance to our coins that we shall not be far from the truth if we
attribute them to the same period.

⅓ Shekels or Didrachms.

WEIGHT.	OBVERSE.	REVERSE.
107·6	City - wall, with four battlemented towers, before which lies an armed galley l. In the exergue are two lions back to back. Border of dots.	Incuse square, within which, the king, crowned, and clad in *candys*, his arms bare, standing l., and seizing with his left hand a rampant lion by the forelock, and about to stab him with a dagger which he holds in his r. Between them an uncertain letter?

[Brit. Mus. Plate II. 7.]

97·9	Another re-struck on a half-shekel of the type of Class 1, No. 2. Of the older type the waves of the sea are visible on the right side of the coin.	Similar. No letter.

[Brit. Mus. Plate II. 8.]

99·4	Similar type; above the city-wall the letter 9.	Similar.

[Brit. Mus. Plate II. 9.]

103·7	Similar type; above the city-wall the letters 90.	Similar; between king and lion 90.

[Brit. Mus. Plate II. 10.]

With these didrachms may be compared a Persian cylinder engraved above, page 34,
where the King is seen killing an ibex in the same way precisely as he kills the lion on
the coins.

The Persian King is also often represented in the Persepolitan sculptures as slaying a monster in the same attitude as upon the coins.

KING KILLING A MONSTER (PERSEPOLIS).

¹⁄₁₂ Shekels or Obols.

WEIGHT.	OBVERSE.	REVERSE.
10·8	City-wall, with three battlemented towers, before which lies an armed galley l. The standard at the stern, as in No. 1 of this class, plainly visible. In ex. lion l.	Incuse square, within which the king, as archer, standing r. and drawing bow, in front of him, the head of a wild goat *incuse* r., and behind him the face of another goat l. also *incuse*, as on No. 2 of Class 1.

[Brit. Mus. Plate II. 11.]

10·8	Same.	Same.

[Brit. Mus. Plate II. 12.]

¹⁄₂₄ Shekel or Hemiobol.

G	City-wall, with three battlemented towers, before which, galley, l.	The king as archer kneeling, in his l. bow, in his r. lance.

[Turin Mus. Found at Aleppo.]

CLASS 3.

PHŒNICIAN STANDARD.

⅓ *Shekel or Drachm.*

WEIGHT.	OBVERSE.	REVERSE.
51·4	Head of goddess (Astarte ?) r. wearing stephane : border of dots.	Incuse square, within which, on a slope, *glacis*, city-wall, with three battlemented towers, behind which two palm-trees.

[Brit. Mus. Plate II. 13.]

¹⁄₁₆ *Shekel or Obol.*

10·6	Similar head.	Incuse square, within which, on a glacis, city-wall, with three battlemented towers, behind which two palm-trees. On the glacis in front of the fortification a wild goat is stretched out *in relief*. Cf. the *incuse* goat on the octadrachms.

[Brit. Mus. Plate II. 14.]

The coins of the above series, 17 in number, although of various types, have much in common, *e.g.* the Goat; which is seen on nine of them, with one exception always incuse; also the fortified city, which is seen on thirteen out of the 17; this last-mentioned type being doubtless a representation of the city where the coins were struck. The galley lying in front of the city-wall shows that this town must have been situated by the sea or on a river; while the Phœnician letters occurring on several specimens, although they have never been satisfactorily explained, some indeed being here given for the first time, would seem to point to the Phœnician coast; and among all the Phœnician towns Tyre is, perhaps, the most probable place of mintage, for her situation on a rocky island, surrounded by a fortified wall, answers to the types of these coins with singular appropriateness.

SERIES II.

The second series of provincial coins in many ways resembles that which has been already described, but the points of divergence are no less clearly marked than those of resemblance.

This series, like Series I., may be divided into several classes, which are to be distinguished by the inscriptions 9, O/1, OO, 9O, and Z˥Z˥.

The coins of these five main classes are all of them clearly later in date than those of Series I.; the specimens are, moreover, generally dated, the dates commencing with year 1 under each separate class. The dates at present recorded are the following:

Class 9	No dates.
,, O/1	Years 1, 3, 13.
,, OO	,, 1, 2, 3.
,, 9O	,, 1, 2, 3, 4, 5, 6, 7, 8, 12, 13.
,, Z˥Z˥	,, 1, 2, 9, 20, 21.

Brandis has suggested that these five classes may correspond with the reigns of the five Kings of Persia, Xerxes B.C. 486–465; Artaxerxes I. 465–424; Darius II. 424–405; Artaxerxes II. 405–359; Artaxerxes III. 359–338, chiefly, I imagine, because in no case do the dates upon the coins transgress the limits of the several reigns.

CLASS 1.

Double Shekels or Octadrachms.

WEIGHT.	OBVERSE.	REVERSE.
426·2	Armed galley with oars advancing l., in the stern a standard surmounted by a disc and crescent, beneath galley, waves; above it ϑ: cable border. [Brit. Mus. Plate II. 15.]	Incuse circle, within which the king with his charioteer in quadriga l., horses walking; behind follows an attendant carrying a one-handled vase and a sceptre or standard ending in an animal's head? Cable border.
430	Similar (no letter). [Brandis, p. 424.]	Similar.

⅛ *Shekel or Didrachm.*

97·3	Armed galley with oars advancing l., in the stern a standard, beneath, waves; above, ϑ: cable border. Above the galley is the Phœnician letter ⅃ꟾ, and in front apparently ε (ʼ ?) both *graffito*. [Brit. Mus. Plate II. 16.]	Similar type.

The Galley on these coins bears in the stern the same standard as the galley which lies before the walls of the fortified town on the coins of Series I. This standard, which consists of a disc surmounted by a crescent, may be compared with a similar one which occurs on a sardonyx inscribed with the name of Abibal, King of Tyre, engraved in de Luynes' Satrapies, pl. xiii. No. 1. The weight of the octadrachms of this class fully comes up to that of the earlier coins—a fact which is conclusive as showing that the coins of this class stand first in the second series. Whether they are Tyrian is doubtful; but that they belong to the Phœnician coast can, I think, hardly be disputed.

¹⁄₁₆ *Shekels or Obols.*

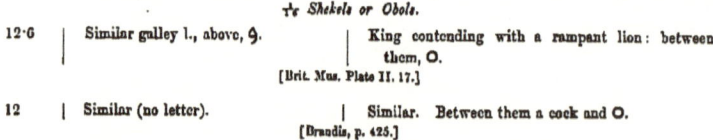

12·6	Similar galley l., above, ϑ. [Brit. Mus. Plate II. 17.]	King contending with a rampant lion: between them, O.
12	Similar (no letter). [Brandis, p. 425.]	Similar. Between them a cock and O.

On those small coins the letter ꒦ on the obverse should perhaps be taken as a portion of the legend ꒦ꂦ or ꂦ꒦, the ꂦ being placed on the other side of the coins.

CLASS 2.

Double Shekels or Octadrachms.

WEIGHT.	OBVERSE.	REVERSE.
393·5	Armed galley with oars advancing l., in the stern a standard, surmounted by a disc and crescent. In the prow an armed man? beneath, waves; above, ꟾ (year 1): border of dots.	The king with his charioteer in quadriga l., horses walking; behind, attendant carrying goat-headed sceptre and vase; above, O/ᛐ: border of dots.
	[Brit. Mus. Plate II. 18.]	
397	Similar. ꟾꟾꟾ (year 3).	Similar.
	[Coll. de Luynes.]	

⅟₁₀ *Shekels or Obols.*

10	Galley l. as above (no date).	Incuse square, within which king contending with lion: between them O/ᛐ ?
	[Brit. Mus.]	
12	Similar. ꟾꟾꟾ⁻ (year 13).	Similar, O/ᛐ.
	[Paris.]	

With this class the weight of the octadrachm falls from about 430 to about 400 grs., and all traces of the incuse square or circle have disappeared on the larger specimens. The interpretation of the Phœnician letters I leave to those who are capable of giving an opinion on the matter; one thing, however, seems certain, that letters which vary on coins otherwise identical, can hardly stand for the name of the city where the coins were struck, unless indeed we presume the existence of a federation of towns using the same coin-types, for which there is no evidence.

CLASS 3.

Double Shekels or Octadrachms.

397·7	Galley as before. Above, ꟾ (year 1).	The king with his charioteer in quadriga l., horses walking; behind, attendant carrying sceptre and vase; above, OO: border of dots.
	[Mus. Luynes.]	
398·2	Similar. ꟾꟾ (year 2).	Similar.
	[Brit. Mus. Plate II. 19.]	
400	Similar. ꟾꟾꟾ (year 3).	Similar.
	[Paris.]	

$\frac{1}{12}$ *Shekels or Obols.*

WEIGHT.		OBVERSE.	REVERSE.
10·1		Similar. II (year 2).	Incuse square, within which king contending with lion; between them OO.

[Brit. Mus. Plate II. 20.]

| 10 | | Similar (no date). | Similar. |

[Coll. de Vogüé.]

CLASS 4.

Double Shekels or Octadrachms.

| 398·5 | | Similar. I (year 1). | Quadriga, etc., as before; above, 9O. |

[Brit. Mus.]

| 398 | | Similar. II (year 2). | Similar [◇O]. |

[Brandis, p. 425.]

| 395 | | Similar. III (year 3). | Similar. |

[Brit. Mus. Plate III. 1.]

| 397 | | Similar. III (year 3). | Similar [ЯO]. |

[Paris.]

| 388·5 | | Similar. IIII (year 4). | Similar. |

[Brit. Mus.]

| 395·9 | | Similar. II III (year 5). | Similar. |

[Brit. Mus.]

| 399 | | Similar. IIII III (year 7). | Similar. |

[Brandis, p. 425.]

| 397 | | Similar. II⁻ (year 12). | Similar. |

[Paris.]

| 395·4 | | Similar. Uncertain date. | Similar. |

[Brit. Mus.]

| 386·5 | | Similar (double struck). | Similar. |

[Brit. Mus.]

$\frac{1}{4}$ *Shekels or Didrachms.*

| 94·8 | | Similar. III (year 3). | 9O. Similar type, no attendant. |

[Brit. Mus. Plate III. 2.]

| 98 | | Similar. IIII IIII (year 8). | Similar. |

[Paris.]

$\frac{1}{8}$ *Shekels or Drachms.*

| 49 | | Similar. I (year 1). | 9O. Similar. |

[Coll. de Luynes.]

| 50 | | Similar. \ sie (year 1). | Similar. |

[Paris.]

HEAD

WEIGHT.	OBVERSE.	REVERSE.
49	Similar. III III (year 6).	Similar.
		[Bank of England. Plate III. 3.]
47	Similar. III IIII (year 7).	Similar.
		[Coll. de Vogüé.]

γ/₆ Shekels or Obols.

10	Similar. II (year 2).	9O King and Lion as before.
		[Brandis, p. 426.]
13	Similar. III (year 3).	Similar.
		[Paris.]
12	Similar. I IIII (year 5).	Similar.
		[Coll. de Laynes.]
10·4	Similar. III⁻ (year 13).	Similar.
		[Brit. Mus. Plate III. 4.]

The coins of this class are more numerous than any of the others. From No. 3 (engraved on Pl. III. Fig. 1), an unusually fine specimen, it appears that the sceptre carried by the attendant is surmounted by an animal's head with long ears of Egyptian style. On No. 1 of Class 2, with O/⌐, it resembles the head of a goat, the beard being clearly visible, with this may be compared the heads of this animal, incuse, on the coins of Series I.

CLASS 5.
Double Shekels or Octadrachms.

396	Similar. Above У.	Quadriga as before, above Z⌐Ζ⁴⌐.
		[Coll. de Vogüé.]
396·7	Similar. Above IУ (year 1).	Similar.
		[Brit. Mus.]
398	Similar. Above IIУ (year 2).	Similar.
		[Coll. de Laynes.]
398	Similar. ЗУ (year 20). This date is accompanied by the letter Λ (graffito).	Similar.
		[Paris. Plate III. 5.]
397·2	Similar. IЗУ (year 21).	Similar.
		[Brit. Mus.]
398·5	Similar. IЗ ? (year 21 ?).	Similar.
		[Brit. Mus.]

γ/₆ Shekels or Obols.

10·5	Similar. III III III (year 9).	King and lion as before, between them Ζ⁴⌐.
		[Brit. Mus. Plate III. 6.]

Weight.	Obverse.	Reverse.
13	Similar. Above [Aramaic letter] and O.	King and lion.
	[Berlin.]	
11	Similar. Above [Aramaic letters].	Similar, between them, cock.
	[Coll. de Luynes.]	

The coins of this class are in many respects different from all which precede, although the types are the same. In the first place, the style of art has become almost barbarous: witness the elongated figure of the king on one of the coins of year 21, where he is enormously out of proportion to the size of the chariot.

In the next place, the fabric is peculiar, the edges of the coins being often hammered flat as on the double darics. The forms of the letters are also different, the Aramaic form [Aramaic letter] taking the place of [Phoenician letter]. The inscription on the reverse [Aramaic letters] has been read מזרי or מזדי. This word occurs frequently on the autonomous coins of Tarsus in the fourth century B.C., and under the Seleucide rule, see Brandis, pp. 500, 501; also on the Satrapal coins of the same city (Brandis, p. 430). But at Tarsus the forms of the characters are somewhat different: [Aramaic letters] instead of [Aramaic letters]. Nevertheless, that these are two forms of one and the same word has been recognized by all (see Waddington, Mélanges, 1861, p. 70; Levy, Phœn. Stud. 1857, p. 40), although all are not agreed as to the meaning of the word. Levy reads it Mazdi (for Ahuramazda). Blau, on the other hand, compares it with the Zend *mizda*, 'pay.' On the obol the word is abbreviated [Aramaic letters]. Brandis looks upon it as equivalent to the Greek ἀργύριον or κόμμα on the silver staters of Seuthes, and this is perhaps, on the whole, the most probable interpretation.

As to the attribution of the coins with this inscription, I am inclined, chiefly on account of their fabric, to doubt whether they are Phœnician, like the coins of the other classes. The types of the widely-circulating Perso-Phœnician coins may well have been adopted by some inland district or city of Syria, possibly Thapsacus, which would fully account for the difference of fabric and for the varying forms of the letters. Thapsacus may also have been in close commercial relations with Tarsus, with which it was connected by the route which passed through Berœa (Aleppo) and the Syrian gates. This would account for the use of the word מזרי on the coinage of the two cities.

Before passing to the next series, we must not omit to mention certain small copper coins, which, by their types, attach themselves to the Perso-Phœnician silver coins of the second series described above. These may be divided into three classes as follows.

CLASS I.

Obverse.	Reverse.
The king and his charioteer in quadriga l., horses walking: border of dots.	Phœnician galley to l.; beneath, waves.

[Brit. Mus. Plate III. 7.]

CLASS II.

OBVERSE.	REVERSE.
The king kneeling r. holding bow in l. and spear in r.: border of dots.	Galley as before.

[Brit. Mus. Plate III. 8.]

Similar.	Similar. ııı (year 3).

[Brandis, p. 549.]

Similar.	Similar. ııı ıı (year 5).

[Brit. Mus.]

Similar.	Similar. ııı ııı (year 6).

[Brit. Mus.]

CLASS III.

Head of king, bearded, r. wearing tiara.	Phœnician galley l.; above, ı⁻ (year 11).

[Brit. Mus.]

Similar.	Similar, ıı⁻ (year 12).

[Paris. Plate III. 9.]

As these copper coins can hardly have been issued before the middle of the fourth century B.C., they afford an indication of the date of the later silver coins, with which they correspond.

It will be well also to notice in this place several other coins, which may be compared with those of Series II. Of these the most remarkable is one of the two didrachms which bear the name of Abd-Hadad. (Brandis, p. 431.)

BAMBYCE.

ATTIC STANDARD.

Didrachm.

WEIGHT.	OBVERSE.	REVERSE.
132	Head of the goddess Atergatis l. with long hair and lofty head-dress. Behind, the date ‏נ‏ (year 30).	‏עבדחדד‏ (Abd-Hadad). The King accompanied by his charioteer in quadriga l.

[Mus. Luynes. Plate III. 10.]

M. Waddington (Mélanges, 1861, p. 90) gives good reasons for attributing this coin to a dynast or satrap of the name of Abd-Hadad, who ruled at Bambyce (Hierapolis) in Syria. The date, year 30, M. Waddington thinks, can only refer to the reign of Artaxerxes Mnemon.

The coin would therefore have been struck in B.C. 375, another indication of the date of the Perso-Phœnician coins of Series II., from which its reverse type is imitated.

There are also two coins in the Hunterian Museum at Glasgow, one of which is of Tarsus, and the other of some Phœnician town, which reproduce the type of the king contending with the lion.

TARSUS.

PERSIAN STANDARD.

Stater.

WEIGHT.	OBVERSE.	REVERSE.
168	The king contending with a rampant lion which he is about to stab with his sword.	The king or a warrior holding a lance in his r. and a crux ansata in his l.; in front, ТЕРΣΙ; behind וחר (תרו) and a flower.

[Mus Hunter. Plate III. 11.]

UNCERTAIN PHŒNICIAN CITY.

Stater.

166	Similar.	ꭓ7Oꝺ. Incuse square, within which is a cow suckling her calf; border of dots.

[Mus. Hunter. Plate III. 12.]

The inscription on this coin remains unexplained, but the forms of the letters point to Phœnicia rather than Cilicia.

The following coin of Tarsus may be also here mentioned, as it bears on its reverse the type of the royal Persian money.

TARSUS.

Stater.

168	Horseman l. holding flower, in exergue וחר?	Incuse square. The king as archer kneeling r.; behind, crux ansata.

[Mus. Hunter. Plate III. 13.]

SERIES III.

The third series of provincial coins with royal Persian types may be divided into two classes according to the standards of weight which the coins respectively follow. These are first Græco-Asiatic and secondly Persian.

CLASS I.

GRÆCO-ASIATIC (RHODIAN SYSTEM).

Staters.

WEIGHT.	OBVERSE.	REVERSE.
216	The king as archer kneeling, r. drawing bow: border of dots.	Horseman wearing the low tiara of the Satraps galloping, r. armed with spear.
	[Brit. Mus.]	
232	Similar.	Similar.
	[Cabinet of M. Six.]	
(?)	Similar; in front O.	Similar.
	[Cat. Behr. No. 851.]	
(?)	Similar; in front OOOX.	Similar.
	[Mionnet. Supp. viii. p. 428, No. 38.]	
232	Similar; in front OO.	Similar; in front star.
	[Munich.]	
230	Similar; in front thunderbolt.	Similar; no symbol.
	[Berlin.]	
224	Similar; behind, Ｙ and lion's head r.	Similar; beneath, bird, r.
	[Cabinet of M. Imhoof-Blumer.]	
223	Similar; no symbol or letter.	Similar; in field ⊙.
	[De Luynes Coll.]	
224	Similar.	Similar; behind, eagle's head.
	[Brit. Mus.]	
227	Similar.	Similar; behind O, beneath, dolphin r.
	[Brit. Mus. Plate III. 14.]	
231	Similar.	Similar.
	[Paris.]	
227·2	Similar.	Similar; behind, a head of Herakles in lion's skin.
	[Brit. Mus. Plate III. 15.]	
259	Similar.	Similar.
	[Imhoof-Blumer.]	

COPPER.

The king kneeling r. holding bow and spear.	Horseman galloping, r. armed with spear.

Size 2 of Mionnet's scale = ·5 inch.

[M. Six. Plate III. 16.]

The silver staters described above are by no means easy to attribute. One valuable indication is however afforded by their weight, which rises as high as 232 grs., and must therefore be considered as of the Rhodian system, which was in use from the year 408, the date of the foundation of Rhodus, until the time of Alexander the Great, throughout the greater portion of the western and south-western coast lands of Asia Minor. We do not find it in Cilicia or in Phœnicia.

It is therefore to the western, or, more strictly speaking, to the south-western, portion of Asia Minor, that I should be inclined to attribute this series of coins, and the *provenance* of some at any rate among them (the island of Calymna) is in favour of this attribution (see Borrell, Num. Chron. o.s. vol. ix. p. 165). In style and fabric they appear to me to be intermediate between those of Class 2 (Pl. III. 17), which, as I shall show, belong to Cilicia, and those of Series IV. (Pl. III. 18–20), which are probably Ionian. In weight they agree with the latter, while in fabric they more nearly resemble the former. They date perhaps from about the commencement of the fourth century B.C.

CLASS 2.

PERSIAN STANDARD.

Stater.

WEIGHT.	OBVERSE.	REVERSE.
163	The king kneeling r., in his l. bow, in his r. lance.	The king kneeling r. holding in his l. bow and with his r. drawing an arrow from a quiver at his shoulder.

[Paris.]

This coin is countermarked with a bull or cow surmounted by two letters generally read IΩ, but perhaps rather |ᴎ.

163	Similar.	Similar.

[Munich. Plate III. 17.]

This coin has two countermarks, one of which is identical with that upon the Paris specimen, while the other contains an eagle and a trident.

161	Similar.	Similar.

[Leake, As. Gr. 80.]

This coin is countermarked with a bull and another animal.

MALLUS.

160·5	The king kneeling r., in his l. bow, in his r. lance.	MAΛ Herakles strangling lion; in field, club.

[Hunter 185.]

The coin is countermarked with a bull and the same two letters.

160·3	Similar.	Similar, in field, grain of corn.

[Leake, As. Gr. 80.]
Same countermark.

Those coins of Mallus fix the attribution to Cilicia of those which bear no inscription. The peculiar countermark, which recurs so frequently, is met with also on other coins of this district, among which may be mentioned four coins of Side in Pamphylia (De Luynes, pl. i., ii. and iii. 5, of 'which last there is another specimen in the British Museum), another coin of Mallus (De Luynes, pl. vi.), one of Soli (Hunter, 51, 30), and one of Celenderis (Brit. Mus.).

The letters over the back of the cow in this countermark have been read IΩ; this Longpérier and De Luynes (p. 6) explain as the name of the cow, Io; the Io legend having been imported into Cilicia by the Argive colonists. For my own part, however, I am disinclined to allow this interpretation of the two letters, because I believe it to be based upon an erroneous reading, for on all the specimens which I have seen with this stamp I read the letters |ᴎ (Γ') and not |Ω.

An Aramaic inscription is moreover more probable on coins of this district than a Greek one, cf. the letters Lᴜy (בעל) over the back of the Bull on a very similar countermark on a coin engraved in De Luynes, pl. ii. 9. But whether we accept or not Longpérier's reading of the two letters, there can be no doubt whatever that the countermark is only found on coins of Cilicia and Pamphylia. To this district therefore we must attribute the coins now under consideration. Their weight also corresponds with that of the coinage of the Cilician coast.

SERIES IV.

The following series of tetradrachms must be distinguished from the preceding, notwith-standing the general similarity of the obverse type.

SILVER.

GRÆCO-ASIATIC STANDARD.

Tetradrachms.

WEIGHT.	OBVERSE.	REVERSE.
229	ΠΥΘΑΓΟΡΗΣ. The king, bearded, crowned, kneeling r. holding bow in l. and spear in r. as on the sigli. [Berlin Mus.]	Incuse square adorned with irregular lumps, the surface granulated.
228	ΠΥΘΑΓΟΡΗ[Σ]. Similar. [Brit. Mus. Plate III. 18.]	Similar.
228	No inscr. Similar. [Brit. Mus. Plate III. 19.]	Similar. •
238·1	Similar. [Brit. Mus.]	Similar, the incuse little if at all granulated.

Weight.	Obverse.	Reverse.
235·7	Similar.	Similar.

[Brit. Mus. Plate III. 20.]

COPPER.

The king kneeling r. as on the darics, drawing bow, behind him IA? Countermarked with star.	Incuse square formed of irregular lumps, the surface granulated.

Size 2½ Mionnet's scale= ·55 inch.

[Brit. Mus. Plate III. 21.]

The king kneeling r. holding bow in l. and spear in r.	Similar.

Size 1 of Mionnet= ·35 inch.

[Brit. Mus. Plate III. 22.]

Similar.	Large square containing a smaller one. On one side of the larger square a straight line joins it at right angles. (Perhaps the representation of a military camp or standard.)

Size 2 of Mionnet= ·5 inch.

[Brit. Mus. Plate III. 23.]

The silver coins of this series are clearly intended as imitations, on a larger scale, of the royal Persian coin, the siglos. The Greek inscription in the Ionic dialect shows that these coins must have been struck in some Greek city, probably in the Ionic Satrapy, subject to Persia, but under the immediate government of a Greek Tyrant or Dynast of the name of Pythagoras. The weight is Græco-Asiatic, not of an early period, but of some time after B.C. 408, about which date the weight of the silver stater was raised in many Greek cities, from about 224 to 236 grs. (Brandis, p. 125). Coins of this heavy weight, as I have before remarked, are never found in Phœnicia or in the East. It may therefore be considered as certain that these interesting Græco-Persian coins were issued after the fall of the Athenian Empire by some Greek city which had again fallen into the hands of the Great King. It is noticeable that the uninscribed specimens reach a higher weight than those with ΠΥΘΑΓΟΡΗΣ.[1]

[1] Vanz's endeavour (Num. Chron. vol. xviii. p. 147) to identify the Pythagoras who issued these coins with his namesake, who engraved an inscription on the base of a column at Sam in honour of his friend Arrencides, strategos of Susiana, may be set aside as purely fanciful. This Pythagoras, who calls himself σωματοφύλαξ, does not make use of the Ionic dialect, and the forms of the letters of the inscription point clearly to the time of Alexander the Great, or his successors the Seleucid kings (see Loftus, Chaldæa, and Susiana, p. 403). The coins, on the other hand, are considerably earlier than Alexander, and by reason of their heavy weight can only be given to the western coast of Asia Minor.

SERIES V.

The coins of this series also belong to the Ionic Satrapy, and may be described as follows:

GRÆCO-ASIATIC STANDARD.

Tetradrachm.

COLOPHON ?

WEIGHT.	OBVERSE.		REVERSE.
236·2	Bearded head of Persian satrap r. wearing the low tiara.	B A ξ Λ I	Lyre.

[Brit. Mus. Plate III. 24.]

HEAD OF PERSIAN KING
(PERSEPOLIS).

The reverse type of this coin, the Lyre, is the Arms, so to speak, of the city of Colophon, where it is most probable that the coin was minted. The head on the obverse is, there can be little doubt, not that of the King of Persia, Artaxerxes Mnemon, whose portrait it is generally considered to be (Waddington, Mélanges, 1861, p. 96), for the Great King always wears the lofty *kidaris* and never the low *tiara*. We must therefore accept the head as that of a Persian satrap. The style of the coin corresponds with that of the time when, after the break-down of the Athenian expedition against Syracuse, the enemies of Athens and of Greek freedom began once more to raise their heads, when Sparta and Persia joined hands, and when orders went forth from the Court of Susa once more to collect tribute from the Asiatic Greeks. It is impossible to speak with greater exactness as to the date of this coin. It is probable however that it is not much later than the year 400 B.C.

GRÆCO-ASIATIC STANDARD.

Tetradrachm.

WEIGHT.	OBVERSE.	REVERSE.
230	Bearded head of Persian satrap r. wearing the low tiara.	Incuse square, within which BAΣIΛEΩΣ, the king bearded, crowned, kneeling r. holding bow in l. spear in r. ; in field l. galley downwards.

[Berlin. Fox. Coll. Plate III. 25.]

Drachm.

52·8	Similar.	BAΣI. Similar, but without galley.

[Brit. Mus. Plate III. 26.]

Obol.

8·9	Same head within a border of dots.	No inscr. same type, border of dots.

[Brit. Mus. Plate III. 27.]

These three coins bear the same portrait as the silver staters of Colophon described above. The reverses have, in addition to the inscription, the well-known 'arms' of the Great King borrowed from the royal darics. The fabric, more especially that of the drachm, seems to be that of the north-western coast of Asia Minor, and it is worthy of note that a portrait of the same satrap, which has been erroneously designated as a portrait of the Great King himself, occurs on a gold stater of Lampsacus (Waddington, Mélanges, pl. vii. 3), and on a silver stater of Cyzicus (De Luynes, i. 5), on which moreover the inscription ΦΑΡ[Ν]ΑΒΑ fixes the attribution beyond a doubt. Pharnabazus is therefore the Satrap whose portrait we possess on the whole of this series of coins, all of which, it may be safely affirmed, date from the last years of the fifth century. The head upon them is that of a man of middle age, and is far more suitable to Pharnabazus shortly before B.C. 400, than to the youthful King of Persia, Artaxerxes II., who ascended the throne in B.C. 405, at the age of nineteen. The bearded figure of the monarch upon the reverse is of course not intended as a portrait; it is merely the arms of Persia, the badge of the supremacy of the Great King.

As it does not form part of my plan to include in the present article any coins but such as bear either the name or the arms of the King of Persia, I pass over the coins of Pharnabazus above alluded to, struck respectively at Lampsacus and Cyzicus, and having on the obverse the portrait of the Satrap, and on the reverse of the one the sea-horse of Lampsacus, of the other the prow of a galley; but the following gold stater, though by its reverse connected with the Cyzicene mint, must not be omitted, since it has on the obverse the royal Persian archer as on the darics.

CYZICUS.

Gold Stater.

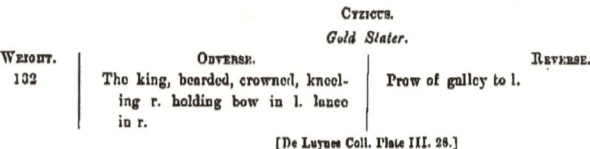

WEIGHT.	OBVERSE.	REVERSE.
132	The king, bearded, crowned, kneeling r. holding bow in l. lance in r.	Prow of galley to l.

[De Luynes Coll. Plate III. 26.]

This unique gold stater clearly belongs to the same period as the silver stater with the name and portrait of Pharnabazus, and is contemporary with the gold coinage of Lampsacus, which, as I have elsewhere shown (Num. Chron. N.S. vol. xvi. p. 288), must be attributed to the end of the fifth and the beginning of the fourth century B.C.

Thus from the earliest invention of the art of coining the precious metals in the middle of the seventh century B.C., in the reigns of Gyges and Ardys in Lydia, I have cast a rapid survey over several classes of coins, Lydian, Persian, Perso-Phœnician, and Græco-Persian, down to the times of the later Achœmenidœ, when the vast empire of Cyrus was already hastening to its fall.

In the Persian portion of my article I have been compelled to limit myself to the description of such coins only as bear unmistakable indications of having been issued under the authority more or less direct of the Great King, commencing with the royal coinage properly so called, viz. the darics and sigli, and then treating of the provincial money with Persian types of Phœnicia, of Syria, of Cilicia, of Ionia, and Mysia, from Tyre and Sidon on the one hand round the south and west coasts of Asia Minor as far as the shores of the Hellespont and the Propontis.

Nevertheless this review of the coinage of Persia is by no means a complete synopsis of the Persian coinage, the important series of the coins of the satraps having been entirely omitted or only infringed upon in those rare instances where the name or effigy of the King of Persia (the word ΒΑΣΙΛΕΥΣ or the royal arms) appears upon the coins conjointly with that of the satrap. The satrapal coinage forms in itself so important a series, and involves so many epigraphical inquiries, that it demands a separate monograph. The great work of the Duc de Luynes, and the still more valuable researches of M. Waddington, have broken the ground and smoothed the path. Herr H. Droysen has also lately contributed to the pages of the Zeitschrift für Numismatik (Bd. ii. pp. 309–319) a suggestive article on the same subject, in which the student of this class of coins will find a useful list of the satraps who coined money both in their own satrapies and in the territory of Cilicia.

INDEX.

TABLE OF THE RELATIVE WEIGHTS OF ENGLISH GRAINS AND FRENCH GRAMMES.

Grs.	Grammes.	Grs.	Grammes.	Grains.	Grammes.	Grains.	Grammes.	Grains.	Grammes.	Grains.	Grammes.	Grains.	Grammes.	Grains.	Grammes.
1	·064	41	2·656	81	5·248	121	7·840	161	10·432	201	13·024	241	15·616	290	18·79
2	·129	42	2·720	82	5·312	122	7·905	162	10·497	202	13·089	242	15·680	300	19·44
3	·194	43	2·785	83	5·376	123	7·970	163	10·562	203	13·154	243	15·745	310	20·08
4	·259	44	2·850	84	5·442	124	8·035	164	10 626	204	13·219	244	15·810	320	20·73
5	·324	45	2·915	85	5·508	125	8·100	165	10·691	205	13·284	245	15·875	330	21·38
6	·388	46	2·980	86	5·572	126	8·164	166	10·756	206	13·348	246	15·940	340	22·02
7	·453	47	3·045	87	5·637	127	8·229	167	10·821	207	13·413	247	16·005	350	22·67
8	·518	48	3·110	88	5·702	128	8·294	168	10·886	208	13·478	248	16·070	360	23·32
9	·583	49	3·175	89	5·767	129	8·359	169	10·951	209	13·543	249	16·135	370	23·97
10	·648	50	3·240	90	5·832	130	8·424	170	11 016	210	13·608	250	16·200	380	24·62
11	·712	51	3·304	91	5·896	131	8·488	171	11·080	211	13 672	251	16·264	390	25·27
12	·777	52	3·368	92	5·961	132	8·553	172	11·145	212	13·737	252	16·328	400	25·92
13	·842	53	3·434	93	6·026	133	8·618	173	11·209	213	13·802	253	16·394	410	26·56
14	·907	54	3·498	94	6·091	134	8·682	174	11·274	214	13·867	254	16·458	420	27·20
15	·072	55	3·564	95	6·156	135	8 747	175	11·339	215	13·932	255	16·524	430	27·85
16	1·036	56	3·628	96	6·220	136	8·812	176	11·404	216	13·996	256	16·588	440	28·50
17	1·101	57	3·693	97	6·285	137	8·877	177	11·469	217	14·061	257	16 653	450	29·15
18	1·166	58	3·758	98	6·350	138	8·942	178	11·534	218	14·126	258	16·718	460	29·80
19	1·231	59	3·823	99	6·415	139	9·007	179	11·599	219	14·191	259	16·783	470	30·45
20	1·296	60	3·888	100	6·480	140	9·072	180	11·664	220	14·256	260	16·848	480	31·10
21	1·360	61	3·952	101	6·544	141	9·136	181	11·728	221	14·320	261	16·912	490	31·75
22	1·425	62	4·017	102	6·609	142	9·200	182	11·792	222	14·385	262	16·977	500	32·40
23	1·490	63	4·082	103	6·674	143	9 265	183	11·858	223	14 450	263	17·042	510	33·04
24	1·555	64	4·146	104	6·739	144	9·330	184	11·922	224	14·515	264	17·106	520	33·68
25	1·620	65	4·211	105	6·804	145	9·395	185	11·988	225	14·580	265	17·171	530	34·34
26	1·684	66	4·276	106	6·868	146	9·460	186	12 052	226	14·644	266	17·236	540	34·98
27	1·749	67	4·341	107	6·933	147	9·525	187	12·117	227	14·709	267	17·301	550	35·64
28	1·814	68	4·406	108	6·998	148	9·590	188	12·182	228	14·774	268	17·366	560	36·28
29	1·879	69	4·471	109	7·063	149	9·655	189	12·247	229	14·839	269	17·431	570	36·93
30	1·944	70	4·536	110	7·128	150	9·720	190	12·312	230	14·904	270	17·496	580	37·58
31	2·008	71	4·600	111	7·192	151	9·784	191	12·376	231	14·968	271	17·560	590	38·23
32	2·073	72	4·665	112	7·257	152	9·848	192	12·441	232	15·033	272	17·625	600	38·88
33	2·138	73	4·729	113	7·322	153	9·914	193	12·506	233	15·098	273	17·689	700	45·36
34	2·202	74	4·794	114	7·387	154	9·978	194	12·571	234	15·162	274	17·754	800	51·84
35	2·267	75	4·859	115	7·452	155	10 044	195	12·636	235	15·227	275	17·819	900	58·32
36	2·332	76	4·924	116	7·516	156	10·108	196	12·700	236	15·292	276	17·884	1000	64·80
37	2·397	77	4·989	117	7·581	157	10·173	197	12 765	237	15·357	277	17·949	2000	129·60
38	2·462	78	5·054	118	7·646	158	10·238	198	12·830	238	15·422	278	18·014	3000	194·40
39	2·527	79	5·119	119	7·711	159	10·303	199	12·895	239	15·487	279	18 079	4000	259·20
40	2·592	80	5·184	120	7·776	160	10·368	200	12·960	240	15·552	280	18·144	5000	324·00

HERTFORD:
PRINTED BY STEPHEN AUSTIN AND SONS.

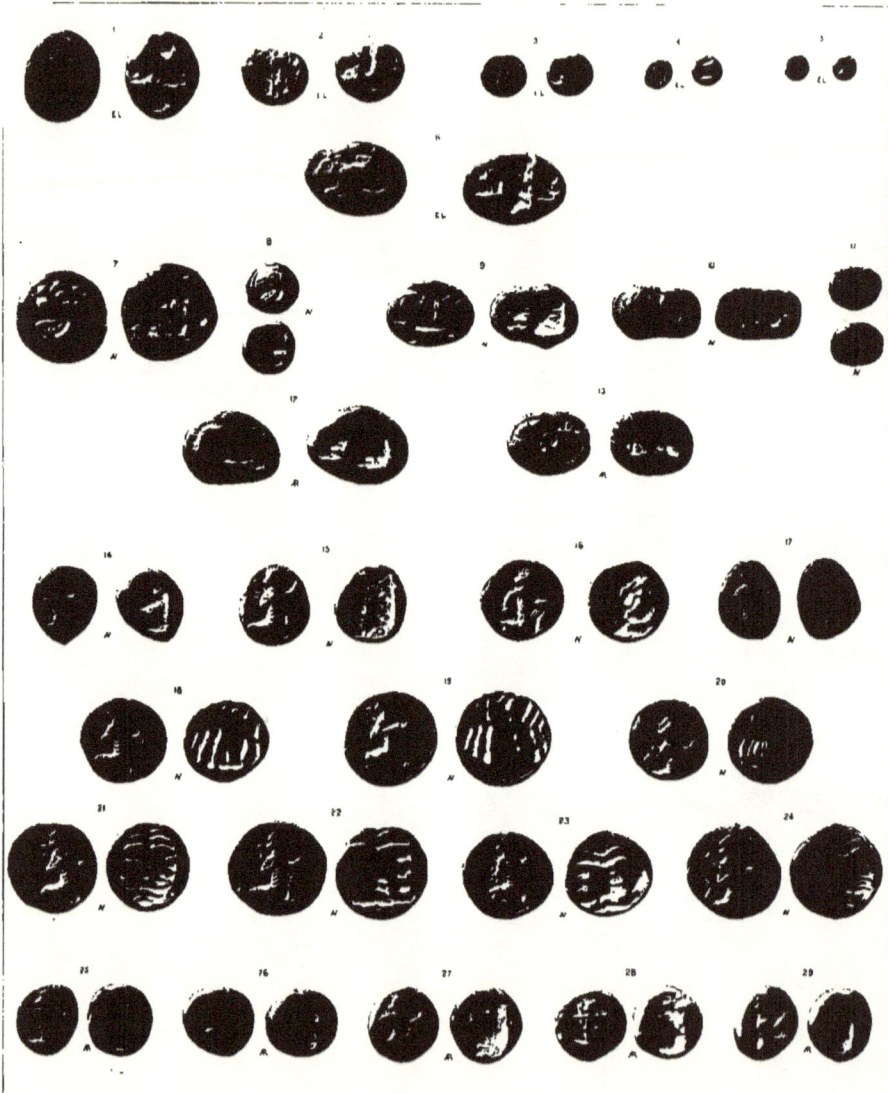

COINAGE of LYDIA and PERSIA.

PLATE. I.

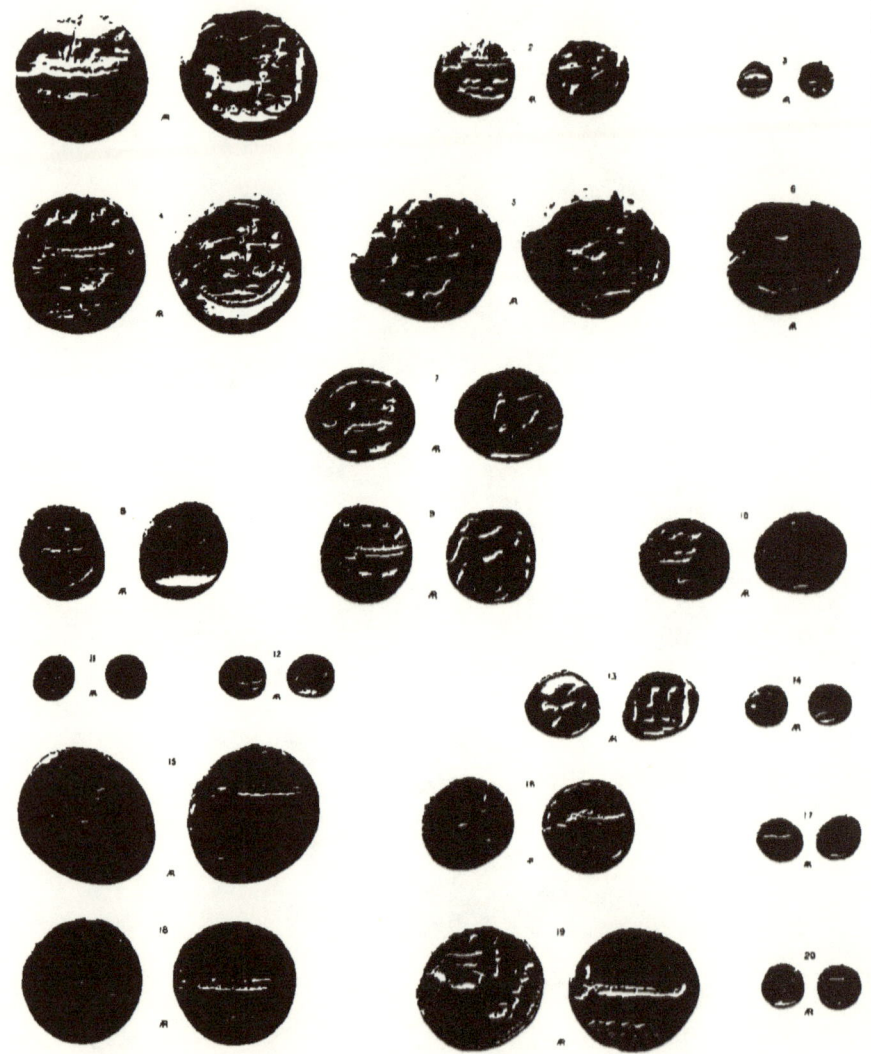

COINAGE OF LYDIA AND PERSIA.

PLATE II.

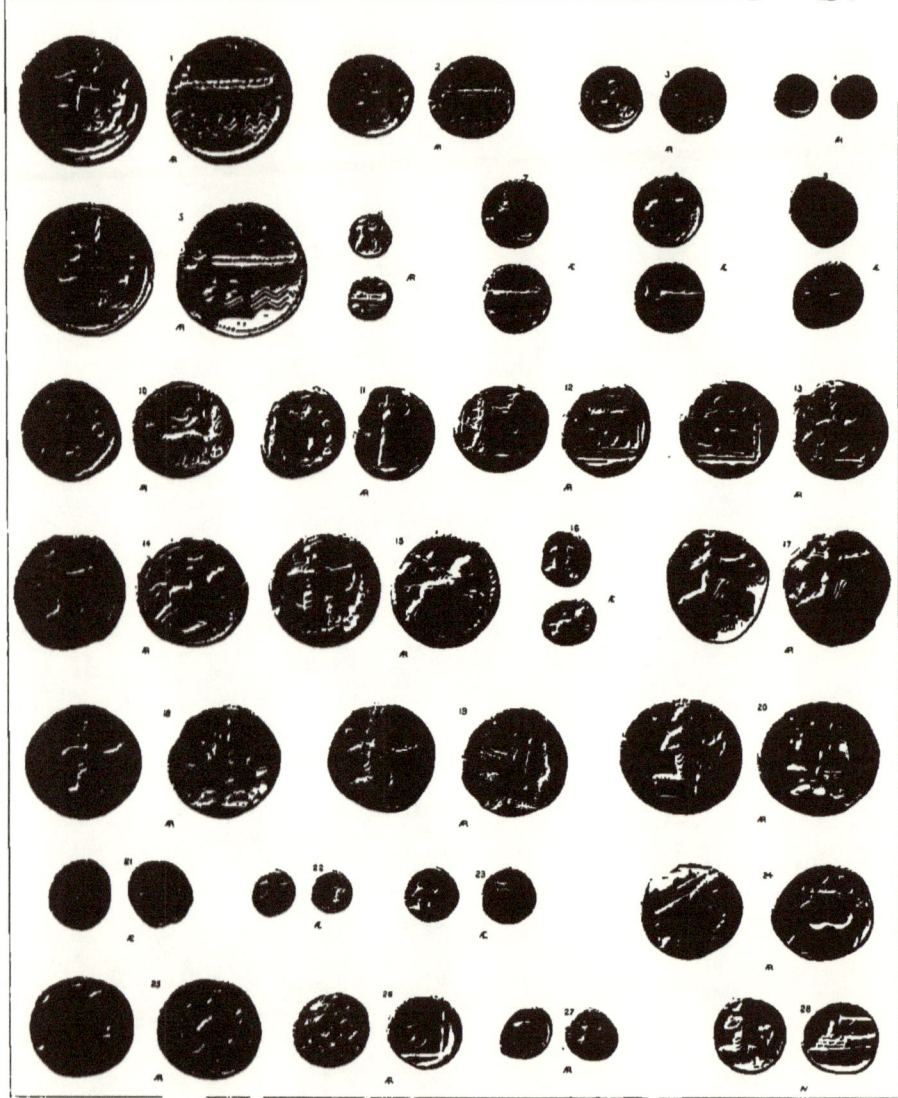

COINAGE of LYDIA and PERSIA.

PLATE III.

THE INTERNATIONAL NUMISMATA ORIENTALIA.

ADVANCED NOTICE.

Since the issue of the tentative prospectus of an International Numismata Orientalia, based upon the original publication of Marsden's Numismata Orientalia, some important modifications of the preliminary plan and general scope of the work have recommended themselves to the Publishers, which have equally commended themselves to the Editor's chief supporters.

The first design comprehended the narrow purpose of the continuation and completion of the substance of the old text published in 1823, with the concurrent reproduction of the admirably executed Copper-plates prepared for Marsden's comprehensive work, which had recently become the property of Messrs. Trübner & Co.

In both these departments the present undertaking henceforth assumes a new and independent form. In lieu of accepting the task of making coins follow and supplement history, it seeks to prove the claims of Numismatic science to a higher mission in the illustration of the annals of olden time, to a power of instruction and teaching where written history is defective, and, in its lowest phase, of testing and rectifying imperfectly preserved facts.

Under this expanded view, therefore, many subordinate sections of Marsden's old work will either be reduced to due proportions in reference to their obsolete form or omitted altogether; while on the other hand a class of subjects uncontemplated in the first International scheme will be introduced and included in this revised programme. For instance, instead of placing the Dynasties of the Khalifs of Baghdád, as of old, at the head of the list, the present monograph refers to the first efforts in the art of coining as exhibited in the electrum and gold pieces of Lydia and Persia. This will be followed by the Phœnician coins of Asia Minor by an eminent German coadjutor. The highly important and specially suggestive series of the Parthian coins has been undertaken, and is now prepared for the press by Mr. Percy Gardner of the British Museum; and Mr. Madden, whose speciality lies in the "History of the Jewish Coinages," will embody in our pages his exhaustive studies in that division of critical numismatics.

General Cunningham's Indo-Scythian series, the materials of which—enriched by the unprecedentedly instructive contents of the late Peshâwar *find*—are arranged and on their way home from India—will now find a fitting introduction in a full and thrice-elaborated review of "the Bactrian successors of Alexander the Great," to which, as a labour of love, he has devoted himself since his first appearance as the chosen Numismatic coadjutor of James Prinsep in 1836.

Secondly, in regard to the illustrations of the old work, which it was once proposed to rely upon: they have been found, however excellent in themselves, practically unsuitable, either in grouping or mechanical accuracy, for the advanced demands of the present day. Indeed, the improved processes by which science has taught us to obtain, at a less cost, absolute *Sun* facsimiles, has necessarily superseded the hand and eye of the engraver, past or present, however perfect in his craft.

As far as the immediate state of the publication is concerned, it may be mentioned as a plea for temporary delay—that, in an amateur work of this kind, there are many obstacles to continuous or periodical issues, and it has been the Editor's aim rather to avoid such publications as were merely mechanical or repetitive; but, on the other hand, there has been no lack of support of the most efficient character, either at home or abroad — indeed, the Editor has had to decline many offers of contributions on the part of Numismatists of established reputation, as our lists are virtually made up beyond any prospect of absence of matter or immediate chance of publication of many of the already accepted papers.

Mr. Rhys Davids' Essay on Ceylon Coins only awaits the completion of the illustrations. Mr. Rogers' paper will appear as Part IV. Sir W. Elliot is well advanced with his contribution; while M. Sauvaire's article has long been ready, under Mr. Rogers' careful translation, but its length has hitherto precluded its publication.

M. de Saulcy is, as of old, ever prepared to come to the front when his aid is called for,—and Dr. Blochmann has already done so much, in the Journal of the Asiatic Society of Bengal, towards the illustration of the local Coinages, that we have merely to reprint his papers whenever the serial arrangement of our articles may call for a consecutive continuation of the Pathán coins of Imperial Dehli. The Editor's own section of the general series is likewise reserved for somewhat similar motives.

M. Gregorieff's completion of his Tátar Dynasties has been deferred during his late duties as President of the Oriental Congress at St. Petersburg. M. Tiesenhausen, whom we might have enlisted and who would willingly join our ranks at this time, has anticipated us in his elaborate survey of "Les Monnaies des Khalifes Orientaux" (1873), which may well claim to constitute *the* standard authority, in its own department, for many years to come. In another division of Numismatics, the Russian savants have been in advance of us, in the publication of the plates of Sassanian coins representing the patient accumulations of 30 years of the life of M. de Bartholomæi (1873—second issue 1875, with an introduction by Prof. B. Dorn). These examples, however, prove less instructive than might have been anticipated. The sameness and iteration of the issues of the Sassanians has always been a subject of remark, but the singular deficiency of important novelties has seldom been so prominently displayed as in this collection, whose representative specimens spread over 32 well-filled 4to. plates.—[E. T.]

SUBJECTS ALREADY UNDERTAKEN, WITH THE NAMES OF CONTRIBUTORS.

Phœnician Coins . . . . DR. JULIUS EUTING, Strassburg.
Coins of the Jews . . . . MR. F. W. MADDEN.
Parthian Coins . . . . MR. PERCY GARDNER, M.A.
Bactrian and Indo-Scythic Coins . . . . GEN. A. CUNNINGHAM, Archæological Surveyor of India.
Coins of the Sassanians of Persia . . . . . . MR. EDWARD THOMAS, F.R.S.
———— early Arabico-Byzantine adaptation . . . M. F. DE SAULCY, Paris.
———— Southern India . . . . SIR WALTER ELLIOT, late Madras C.S.
———— Ceylon . . . . MR. RHYS DAVIDS, late Ceylon C.S.
———— Arakan and Pegu . . . . SIR ARTHUR PHAYRE, late Commissioner of British Burmah.
———— the Khalifs of Spain, etc. . . . . DON PASCUAL DE GAYANGOS, Madrid.
———— the Fatimites of Egypt . . . . M. H. SAUVAIRE, Cairo.
———— the Túlún Dynasty of Egypt . . . . MR. E. T. ROGERS, Cairo.
———— the Ikhshídís . . . . MR. REGINALD STUART POOLE, Keeper of Coins, B.M.
———— the Seljuks and Atábeks . . . . MR. STANLEY L. POOLE, C.C.C., Oxford.
———— the Bengal Sultáns . . . . DR. H. BLOCHMANN, Calcutta.
———— the Russo-Tátar Dynasties . . . . PROFESSOR GREGORIEFF, St. Petersburg.